PLAIN JANE

KIM HOOD grew up in Canada, but now lives in the west of Ireland with her partner and daughter. She has an eclectic background in education, therapy and social services, which hasn't helped her one bit in her latest endeavours of smallhold farming and running a local newspaper. *Plain Jane* is her second novel. Her first novel *Finding A Voice* was nominated for the YA Book Prize in 2015.

PLAIN JANE

When does being stuck
become ... unstuck?

From the author of *Finding A Voice*

KIM HOOD

SHORTLISTED FOR THE YA BOOK PRIZE 2015

THE O'BRIEN PRESS
DUBLIN

First published 2016 by
The O'Brien Press Ltd,
12 Terenure Road East,
Rathgar, Dublin 6,
D06 HD27, Ireland.
Tel: +353 1 4923333;
Fax: +353 1 4922777
E-mail: books@obrien.ie.
Website: www.obrien.ie

ISBN: 978-1-84717-784-1

8 7 6 5 4 3 2 1

20 19 18 17 16

Cover image courtesy of iStockphoto
Printed and bound by Nørhaven Paperback A/S, Denmark.
The paper in this book is produced using pulp from managed forests

DEDICATION

This book is for Karl – who helps me to see the beauty that is everywhere, and reminds me to look for it within. The world would be a colourless place without him.

ACKNOWLEDGEMENTS

Thank you to: my editor, Helen – who saw the kernel of what really mattered in this story far before I did; my agent, Svetlana – who I trust to never lie to me; Emma – for her beautiful design; my ever-patient family and friends (both close and far) – who put up with so much time stolen from them in the writing of this one; to Toby and Steve for allowing me a space to hide away in and write for days on end; and to Johnny Cash (the cat, not the singer) who kept me company there. And now that I know how much goes into a book both before and after it heads out into the world: thank you so much to everyone at The O'Brien Press for your enthusiasm and support.

GRAVE MORENDO

'VERY SLOW, DYING'

I didn't even knock on the basement window before sliding it open and tumbling through, to land on the sagging sofa beside Dell.

'Jesus, Jane,' Dell said. 'Can't you use the front door like someone normal?'

Dell hadn't yet turned on the lamp beside him, and with the fading light trying in vain to find its way in through the ground level window, the basement room was dark already. Dell was sitting where he always was, video controller between his thumbs. He hadn't even paused the game.

'I don't like to run into your dad upstairs. He'll be up any minute. He is on nights, right?'

You might say that Dell's dad and I have never warmed to each other. In a small village, you never 'meet' parents for the first time, because usually you have at least seen them around all of your life, but it was still different to meet Alan as Dell's dad and not just Alan-who-drives-the-red-Chevy. Dell and I had walked into the kitchen while his dad was eating breakfast – at four o'clock in the afternoon. I'd grabbed my history textbook before following Dell up the stairs. I guess the text was a kind of 'parent pleasing' prop, like it would suggest that I was doing homework downstairs.

Alan had looked me up and down in a way that pretty

8

much creeped me out. It wasn't a 'are you good enough for my son?' look, put it that way. I didn't seem to meet his approval in the other way either though, as he had turned his attention back to the television on the counter before even saying hello. Not that he greeted Dell either.

Dell hadn't seemed phased by that though, walking around his dad to get to the fridge without a word to him. While he went about pouring us glasses of cola, and opening cupboards looking for anything to eat, I just stood there by the table, hugging my stupid *20th Century World History* textbook. Alan just kept watching the TV, which made me feel awkward. When I get nervous I can't stay still, so I had to start running my thumb across the page ends of my book, which made it slip out of my hand. My dive to catch it had only succeeded in knocking it further – right where Dell's dad's full cup of coffee was. So much for parent pleasing.

While I tried to mop up most of the coffee from the table and the textbook, Dell's dad had just watched me.

'So you're a smart girl, are you?' he said, and I wasn't sure if he was referring to the textbook or the fact that I had just ruined it, and his cup of coffee to boot, until he went on. 'You're wasting your time with Dell, then. He may be pretty, but he isn't too bright.'

What was I supposed to say to that? It wasn't a joke either. No one laughed. Worse, Dell didn't seem to even be embarrassed by the comment. There aren't many things people can

say that I don't have a smart comeback for. In fact I have a
tendency to open my mouth without thinking, even when I
shouldn't. That though, shut me up.

'It isn't like he doesn't know you're here,' Dell said now.
His shoulder bumped mine, but it wasn't a greeting; his car
on the screen just happened to be taking a sharp turn to the
right, and he followed it with a lean in that direction. He
was right of course. There were not many nights I wasn't
here. Dell's dad might not have cared, but there was a time
when my parents would have given me serious grief for even
thinking about being in the house with a guy with no adults
around.

'Yes, but if we don't *see* one another, we can *pretend* I'm
not here.' I gave Dell a shove and reached over for the bag of
chips in front of him. 'It's an agreement we have.' I thought it
might be an agreement that Dell had with his dad as well. I'd
seen Dell and his father in the same room of their two-floor
duplex only a handful of times in all the while we had been
going out, with no more talk between them than that first
day. And that was not many times, given that it felt like Dell
and I had been together forever.

Dell kept up his furious driving through the streets of Sin
City. I waited to see whether he would ask me about my
day; I knew he wouldn't. I was glad he wouldn't really, but I
wasn't going to let him off so easily either.

'I had a smashing day; thanks for asking, Dell. And how

about you? Any scintillating news from the gas station? Did you put enough money into the pockets of the multinationals?' I had to nudge him again before he registered that I had asked him a question.

'Huh? It was alright.' He paused the game and looked at me with that wide-open smile he has, the one that would disarm any girl. 'Susan is going to give me full-time hours when Linda goes off to have her baby.'

I wanted to make some wisecrack about being glad that he had climbed to such dizzying heights on the ladder to success, but I didn't. I could see he was genuinely proud of himself. Dell doesn't have a lot of confidence at the best of times, though most people don't know that. I didn't know that until we got together.

He'd been two years ahead of me in school, and by the time I started high school in town he had established himself as cool. He was good at every sport, and that matters a lot around here. Plus he is that sort of good looking that makes every girl want to be near him, but without any of the bad-boy look to him. I think me and my friend Tracey spent all of eighth grade secretly swooning over him.

That was before he quit school. Not that quitting school was earthshattering or anything – lots of guys here do it because they can get a job in the mine without graduating. But with Dell, he just didn't go back after grade 10. He doesn't talk about it, and his dad never questioned it at all.

I'm sure Alan thinks Dell was just too stupid to do grade 11 – and so even Dell doesn't really believe his dyslexia had anything to do with his bad grades. I guess it was easier to just quit.

Maybe it was that the only light now was the blue glow from the screen, but looking at him, I could see what he would look like at forty – still little-boy cute, only with a bit of a gut and a v of forehead reaching back from each temple. Would he be sitting on this same sofa? Would I be sitting beside him? Would he be just home from his full-time job at the gas station?

I pushed the image away and took the video-game-free-moment to give him a hug. Someone had to congratulate him, and nobody else in this house was going to do it. His dad was too busy living the dream – working shifts at the mine and filling his shed with empty Budweiser cans. Just like half the town.

'How's Emma?' He didn't always ask; Dell wasn't one to go looking for bad news.

'Maintaining that fighting spirit that everyone is so fond of talking about.' In truth, when I'd left her two hours ago, she'd been sucking on ice, because it was the only thing that wasn't coming back up. The room had reeked of puke.

Dell definitely didn't want to hear about that though. Nobody did. Everyone held fast to the image of ten-year-old Emma-Rose, dressed in a frilly pink tutu, dark brown curls framing her pixie face. Never mind that the photo on the dog-eared poster, appealing for donations for 'our angel', was three years out of date.

My little sister wasn't always a living angel. Once she was a normal, sometimes annoying, always there (the way a chair in the sitting room has always been there and you don't even think about whether it should be or not) part of the family. To tell you the truth, I never thought much about her before 'The Diagnosis', and ever since, I have been trying my best to think even less about her. That is rather difficult though, as the world tends to love a Living Angel. At least, that is my experience.

Not that my experience is that broad, mind you. The official population of my village, Verwood, is 423 – give or take the few who swear they're leaving for good and never coming back, and then do within six months.

Anyway, maybe it's because we live in such a small place that 'The Diagnosis' focused so much attention on one child. I mean, if we lived in a big city like New York or Paris or probably even Kamloops, nobody would have noticed as much. There must be millions of sick kids. Well, maybe not millions, but thousands at least.

Here, Emma-Rose (and by the way, nobody called her that until 'The Diagnosis' – it was just plain Emma before that) is something of a phenomenon. People talk about her being an Inspiration, an Example of Hope, an Angel (thus the Living Angel theme I started with). But I know what they really wish for. They want her to die, so that she can be representative of something.

I'm not sure what. I'm only fifteen and not exactly a genius. I'm not even a driven, full-of-potential kind of fifteen-year-old. I'm a class-skipping, pot-smoking (well not really, but no one in my town would care if I was), hangout-in-my-boyfriend's-basement-playing-video-games kind of fifteen-year-old.

Don't get me wrong. I'm not some jealous, left out sister, who is on the way to ruining her life. I actually really love my sister. I used to really love my whole family – when there was a 'whole' to love. Now there's just me, and there's Dad, and if there's any unit at all in the four of us, then it's Mom and Ems. But that is only because they're the only ones who spend any time together these days. I guess they have to. It's not like you can leave a sick kid by herself in the hospital day after day.

So I get it. That's the way it is. That's the way it has been for nearly three years. I'm kind of done crying about it.

But when I looked over at Dell, I couldn't help feeling like I was drowning a little. Drowning in this ... waiting. This nothingness that had become my life.

So no, I was definitely not on the way to ruining my life. That would have been a whole lot more exciting.

When I turned onto our street, our house stood out like a missing tooth; it was the only one in complete darkness, even though it wasn't quite 9.00pm, even though Dad's truck was parked in the driveway. At least in darkness you couldn't see the pale blue paint peeling to reveal the ugly green that Mom had insisted on painting over before she would even move in.

Poor house. It wasn't getting much attention these days. Mom had been mumbling for weeks, every time she navigated her way through the overgrown shrubs at the front and had to wade through the grass bending over the cement walkway, that she was going to cut the grass *this* weekend. Well, *this* weekend wasn't going to be until next year now; the ground was frozen solid. At least this year there weren't still Halloween decorations hanging in the front windows weeks after the event. We hadn't even bothered to put any up. There hadn't seemed to be much point since we'd known that Emma would be back in the hospital by Halloween.

Dad was exactly where I thought he would be, on the sofa, stinking wool socked feet resting on the coffee table in front of him, mouth open, asleep. He'd obviously worked a double shift again. I felt a finger of guilt spread from my gut, seeing him so worn out like that. I should have come straight home from the hospital and made some dinner for us. That was it. From now on I was going to get it together and start making meals; at least on some of the nights Mom wasn't coming home.

How many times had I thought this? I *meant* to be more of a help. I mean, there wasn't too much reason why I couldn't have mowed the freaking lawn for my mother. Or done a bit of laundry, or done anything at all to help. I just couldn't seem to organise myself to actually follow through.

And the ironic thing? Nobody ever gave me a hard time about doing nothing. Nobody said anything at all about it. 'Before the Diagnosis' there is no way I would have gotten away with how little I do. Both Mom and Dad have this ridiculously strong work ethic and it has been their mission in life to drill it into their daughters as well. I'd always hated how Emma gave into it. She'd always made me look twice as bad when I had refused to submit to slave labour easily. She had left me to fight the battle for both of us, while she remained the good one.

'Give it a rest, Mom, will you?' I remember saying when she came into my room to complain about the mess, and to order me to clean it up immediately. 'It's not like I don't know how to clean it. I'll do it; just not on your timetable.'

'If you know so much about how to clean, why is it absolutely never done?'

'Like I said – my timetable. Summer 2017.'

Who knew that all it would take was a dose of cancer for

my protest against chores to end successfully?

Only, now I could do with a little of that conflict. It turns out I can't seem to get it together without nagging.

Soup. I could heat up some soup for Dad.

I almost lost hope of doing even that though when I walked into the kitchen. The counter all around the sink was cluttered with dirty dishes. With Emma spewing her guts the last few days, Mom hadn't made it home at all, and well, I just told you how much I have been doing lately in the house-keeping department. And Dad was practically not here at all.

I lifted the fry pan, still covered with congealed bacon grease from Sunday's breakfast and found a pot that didn't need too much of a scrub. I tried not to look at the bits of food at the bottom of the sink. It reminded me of this after-noon.

It had been my job to hold the cardboard vomit-catcher today, while Mom took a break down in the cafeteria. I had known it was a bad day the minute I came into Emma's room. She was watching the DVD of Grandad again.

I would really like to stomp on that DVD until it was only tiny shreds of plastic. It is the most ridiculous piece of cin-ematography ever made.

I know it by heart at this stage, and you really do have to hear the entire spiel to appreciate how utterly horrible it is. Here is how it goes:

[Enter Grandad, tubes coming out of his nose, walking

PLAIN JANE

with a cane, taking a seat behind his giant, some-sort-of-professional-career desk that was the place we most often saw him at, before he got too sick to work.] But now I am digressing from the script.

[He clears his throat, lays his hands upon the desk, and throws his shoulders back.]

'Emma-Rose [even he gave in to the sentimentality of calling Emma that, the most unsentimental man I knew], you know that I am not a sentimental man [see, told you], and so I will not give you sentiment here. But you are a remarkable young girl, with a gift. When you dance, I want to dance with you.'

Are you getting the picture? I don't think I can go through the entire thing. It makes me nearly as ill as Ems was today to think about it.

[Skip to the end of the video.]

'And so there is only this to say to you, sweet granddaughter: fight, fight hard. I love you more than I ever thought possible [I think this bit was in reference to skipping out on his wife and daughter – who happens to be my mom – and basically not getting back in touch for twenty years, until Emma and I came along]. I may not be here at the end of the fight, but you will be.'

I cannot believe that Mom lets Emma watch that video over and over again. I mean, it can't be only me who thinks it is ludicrous for a dying man to give an inspirational speech to a little girl. I don't even know how Mom forgave him for leaving her and Grandma when she was only six. I would certainly not have forgiven him. Nor would I have let him give my impressionable daughter a sick video about how to beat cancer with a bit of 'rah, rah, let's get better'.

Here I am, going off on a complete tangent. I tend to do that. It entertains me. God knows, this town is short on entertainment.

So yes, it was a bad day. Capital B, bad day. But then, days around our house range from 'hey, it could be worse' to 'it can't possibly be worse'.

Even on the bad days, Emma is nice to everyone. She knows I hate that video, so she had turned off the laptop when I came in. The effort to sit up and do that had been almost too much for her and she'd left her arm hanging off the side of the bed while she curled the rest of her body into a ball.

'Do you mind if I pop out for a coffee, Jane?' Mom had asked. She had her purse on her lap, ready for the minute I arrived. It didn't look like she had even brushed her hair today. She didn't have any make-up on. There was a time when she would not have been caught dead without it.

'I'd say you need more than one, Mom.'

Mom had barely given Emma a reassuring kiss and left the room before Emma started to retch, trying to reach for the cardboard bowl herself.

'Hold on, Ems. I've got you.' There was at least something I could do on days like today – hold my little sister's impossibly thin shoulders while her body protested what the drugs were doing to her in the only way it could. I couldn't even hold her hair back anymore. She didn't have any to hold back.

After the first bout was over, Emma had laid back, exhausted from a day of it. There was a trail of sick down one arm of her fleece pyjama top, a top she had had for two years and not grown out of yet.

'I'm sorry, Jane.' She is always apologising.

'You should be. No self-respecting thirteen-year-old wears pyjamas with teddy bears on them.' I took off my own hoodie and unhooked her drip, manoeuvring the line through arm holes until she was wearing the hoodie instead. I had to roll the sleeves up for her.

'Do you think Mom will let me go to the high school when I'm done here?' she had asked out of the blue. Sometimes I hate that Emma is so optimistic. Sometimes I think it should be me lying in that bed.

I'm not though, and Dad still had to eat, so I opened a can of tomato soup and even managed to find some ham and cheese to make him a sandwich as well. When I took it out to him, he hadn't changed positions at all.

'Dad.' I gave him a shake. And then another, until he finally opened his eyes and sat up.

'I did it again, didn't I? Fell asleep before I could make dinner,' he said. 'I think it must be this chair that puts me to sleep.'

'Definitely the chair,' I said, 'because it couldn't have anything to do with working sixteen hours straight.'

Dad would have smiled at that once, but now his expression never wavered from weariness. He just heaved himself out of the chair and padded to the table, like he was a five-year-old, and I was his mother, just waking him from his nap. Where Mom had become nicer, in a weird absent way, Dad had just become a cardboard cut-out of himself. It's like he hardly existed anymore. Sometimes I felt like doing more than shaking him awake; sometimes I wanted to scream at him, just to see if he would scream back.

It kind of just took too much energy though, so instead I went back in to get myself some soup as well, even though I wasn't even hungry. And then we ate in silence, like we always do these days. We'd given up on the small talk a while ago.

'Well, I better get to my homework,' I said, when my bowl was empty.

Dad didn't ask why it wasn't done yet. He didn't ask where I'd been all evening. For all I knew he hadn't even noticed I wasn't there before he collapsed in a heap in his chair.

I'm not sure exactly when I decided to make school an optional part of my day. I'm not sure exactly why I made this decision either. If I am totally honest, then I didn't decide at all. It just started to happen.

Emma started to get sick the same month I started secondary school, but it didn't really interfere with my life for a while. I wasn't even around enough to notice. Obviously in a village of 423 there aren't enough kids to populate a whole secondary school, so I took the bus, with everyone else in Verwood, to Kendal – forty-five minutes away. This is another fantastic thing about living in a backwoods village – donating an hour and a half of your life to sitting on a bus every day for your entire high school life.

So it didn't matter that Mom and Emma were spending all of their days in Red River, a further half hour away, while doctors tried to figure out what was wrong with her. I mean, I am not a complete callous bitch, of course it *mattered* that Emma was not well, but it wasn't like all of a sudden I was the left out child, pining for my mother's attention or anything. I was in school or on the bus the whole time these appointments were happening – nothing to do with me. Hell, once in a while the appointments even worked out so that Mom could pick me up from school.

It just happened that things were changing in our family at the same time things were changing for me as a person. It was coincidence, that's all. I was almost thirteen. I'd say things would have changed even without Em's diagnosis.

I'm rambling, I know. What I mean is – I didn't start skipping school because Emma was sick. I wasn't in some sort of emotional upheaval; it wasn't a cry for help or anything. I just started to not want to go. Simple.

I guess somewhere in there Grandad got sick too, and even though he wasn't *really* sick yet, Mom kind of hinted a lot that it would be nice for me to go up the hill to his house on some of my lunch hours, just to say hello. Sometimes taking a class off before lunch, to get up the courage for an awkward hour with him, seemed like a good idea. Sometimes, taking a class off to recover from an awkward hour with him also seemed like a good idea.

I say all of this because in the early days of missing school I had this ridiculously nice school counsellor try to say that the two things – Emma's illness and me skipping school – were related.

I guess I'd been leaving school early for a couple of weeks, not every day, but quite a few days, before I got pulled out of my first class. Even the way she came to the door of my English class was nice.

'You wouldn't mind if I borrowed Jane for a few minutes, would you Mr Smith?' she'd asked, after knocking softly and opening the door. And then all of the way down the hall to her sort-of office she had kept turning around and smiling at me, as I trailed behind her, wondering what my punishment was going to be. It had been a bit of a buzz actually. I'd never been in trouble at school in my life before. Could they kick me out?

But she was still smiling when we got to her sort-of office. I say sort-of office, because even though it had her name on the door 'Eva Hartigan — Counsellor', like it was an office, inside it was more like she had moved her living room into the school. There was a little couch and a matching chair—all poufy, so you sunk right down when you sat. And it was like the place had been professionally decorated — with accents that were all lime green and that blue that isn't quite tur-quoise. I can tell you, that decorating definitely didn't come out the publically funded budget. Eva had spent her own money on kitting the place out.

Instead of being inviting though, it pretty much screamed 'desperate to be taken seriously as a professional'. As soon as she opened her mouth I knew why she needed the decor.

'So, welcome, Jane,' she started. 'I want you to feel at home. Do you know why I've asked you here?' Somehow, when she said anything, it seemed like she was reading it from a script.

'I don't suppose it's because I've won a prize for 'Best Hair of the Week' is it?' I told you, I was feeling a bit bold, and this woman evoked rebellion. She just kept going though.

'So we both know that things have been slipping a little for you, haven't they, Jane?' She was still smiling, that kind of smile you save for people you don't know, but who you really need to like you. Like maybe a dentist that is about to perform dental surgery, while you are asleep, so you definitely want him to like you, so he remembers you are more than just a surgery candidate.

Only I was just a twelve-year-old kid at the time. I should have been afraid of her, not the other way around.

'Slip sliding away.' The lyrics to the song had popped into my head, and I hadn't been able to resist speaking them aloud.

'Pardon?'

'Nothing, sorry, never mind.' It occurred to me, a little too late mind you, that I had better respond to her as if she was in control, even if it wasn't true.

'Jane, you've had an awful tragedy at home, and it's perfectly normal to want help, but not know how to ask for it.'

'Have I had an awful tragedy? I wasn't aware that anyone had died.'

She went a little red at that.

'No, no, of course not,' she said. 'But I am sure it must be difficult. Your Mom is very busy with your sister, just when you are entering a new period in your life.'

That had struck me as kind of funny – only because I had just started my period that day. Not for the first time of course; it wasn't *that coincidental,* but it was still funny. I don't think I actually laughed, but I definitely smiled. Poor Eva; she didn't know what to do with that. She kind of sputtered. I think she had been prepared for me to burst into tears. There was even a big box of tissues (one with blue and green swirls adorning it, though not quite the right shade of blue to match the room) in a very prominent place, at the ready.

I tried to help her out then. I don't exactly like to make people upset, even though sometimes I say things, or react in ways, that does just that. I adopted a more sombre expression, concentrating on feeling sad.

'It isn't the most cheerful time in my house.' I would give her that; there had been this weird tension at home for weeks, with everyone doing exactly what they usually did, only with plastic grins and ending sentences in an inflection that was just a little too high to be natural. 'But hey, every dancer goes through some injury time, don't they?'

See, at the time when Emma got diagnosed with cancer, when she finally did, after weeks of tests – nobody told me. Everyone knew except me. Even Emma knew. When I asked what was going on, I got vague answers about the strain of excessive training on young ligaments. But of course I *did* know. The plastic grins made it pretty obvious that something more was going on.

So I suppose I wanted someone to tell me directly.

But this counsellor was not going there. She was a 'play-it-safe' kind of professional, and she had learned her catch phrases well.

'Sometimes when we suffer an upset, instead of talking about it, we start withdrawing from things, even activities we enjoy.'

'Uh huh? Like what activities? Flower arranging?' I couldn't believe that she wasn't just going to name it – that I was skipping classes.

That did get her though. She gave a little sigh before saying, 'Jane, not going to classes is not going to help the situation with your sister. It isn't going to make you feel better. It's just avoidance.'

'Okay.' There had been nothing else to say. It had felt like we were having two different conversations at the same time, or like she was talking to someone else who wasn't me. I didn't see how not going to math class, for an example, because we were going to be learning about quadratic equations say, that didn't interest me at all, had anything to do with Emma.

'So you will come to talk to me, instead of just leaving school?' There had been a hopeful look to her then. Maybe counsellors get paid on commission or something – the more kids they convince to listen to their 'wisdom', the more money they make. 'My door is always open, and you are welcome to just come in to hang about if you want.'

'Sure, Eva.' She hadn't introduced herself; I could have been overstepping the mark by not using her last name, but I wasn't; she smiled like I had just given her a present.

That was over three years ago and I hadn't seen Eva in over two of those years. At first I had popped in once in a while. I hadn't stopped skipping classes, but there isn't a lot to do in Kendal, and people would kind of look at me suspiciously if I hung around any one store for too long. Then it got cold of course, so having a place to hang out that wasn't in the snow was a bonus. Plus, she had those really comfortable chairs. She wasn't even such bad company once she stopped trying to counsel me.

But then, for some reason I just stopped going. I think it was around the time that Grandad got sicker, and probably it was the time when Emma started having to stay in the hospital for weeks instead of days. I'd probably had legitimate reasons to be out of school, checking on Grandad or going to the hospital to see Emma. To be honest, it seems like a long time ago.

I just know she didn't last the year without being chewed up and spat out by some tougher cases than me. She started to need some of those tissues on her desk after one of the tenth grade boys started spreading a rumour about what she had gotten up to on her sofa with him. And then one day she wasn't there anymore. And there wasn't a replacement councillor. So maybe she did use public funds to decorate her office after all, and the money was all gone when they went to hire a new one.

So now, I get called into the principal's office every month or so. For a chat. You would not believe it, but I have never so much as gotten a suspension for skipping. I know Mom and Dad have received a few letters, and I think Mom has even managed to go in to talk to the school the odd time, but I've never received any real grief.

I guess I keep my head down just enough. I haven't failed anything yet, put it that way. Teachers have more than me to worry about. I'm getting by.

Besides, with Emma in the hospital so much of the time, I usually have the excuse of not being in school because I could be there with her, which technically, is very feasible. The 1pm bus to Red River is way more direct than the one at 3:30. The one at 3:30 takes nearly forty-five minutes and so I only have about an hour and a half at the hospital before I have to catch the 6 o'clock bus back home on the days that Mom stays overnight with Emma, which seems like all of the time lately.

But the truth is, I don't take the earlier bus most days. An hour of time at the hospital is almost too much for me to stand. More and more I feel like a stranger when I am there anyway. Emma and Mom seem to have this routine and way of not even talking and yet knowing what the other is thinking. And I am just … there in the corner. Sometimes I sit there not saying or doing anything to see when they will notice. They don't.

I sometimes wonder if things would have been different if Emma hadn't have gotten sick. When we were kids I never thought of Emma as being a friend; she was just my little sister. But now, with her not home most of the time, it feels like I'm missing something. Not exactly a friend, but the *potential* for a friend. I'm missing closeness that we haven't had a chance to find.

Mostly though, I think things would have been the same as now. Not the same as in hanging out in the corner of a hospital room, but Mom-and-Emma-being-a-closed-unit kind of the same. Honestly though, as much as I used to complain about everything being about Emma's dancing, I know she was really good – like professional-potential good, that was heading toward way more than a couple of lessons a week and a recital twice a year. That kind of good that requires everyone else to come second. I never said it, but I was so proud of her that it seemed worth it, being on the outside of that.

But this? This never-ending survival, with no end date? This feels so pointless.

All of this explanation is to say that even as I was getting on the bus in the morning, I'd decided that it was going to be a two-class day. I divided up my school days into zero-class days, two-class days – where I left at the first break, three-class days – until lunch, and five-class days. Basically, at this point, five-class days were mostly those that ended in a class that didn't require much from me, or days when either I forgot to leave or where the weather was too bad for me to want to bother going out into it. Any day that I was going to the hospital was never more than a three-class day.

Nobody else seems to know my system though.

'Hey, stranger,' Tracey greeted as I slid into the seat beside her. 'Are you around for lunch?'

Tracey is kind of my best friend. She is getting a bit of a bad deal lately though. She has to ask this every day, even though she doesn't always get an honest answer, because she is the most loyal person I know. Even though I basically am never there for her when she needs me, she always, always puts me first, which means that if I am around for lunch, she'll hang out with me; if I'm not, she defaults to her second choice of hanging out with Brenda and Aishling. They don't want much to do with me since I inadvertently insulted everything they hold dear. It really was not intended; I'd thought we had all been talking tongue-in-cheek. Apparently it was only me that had been.

It was at lunch time. We'd been sitting around nursing our fries, which is what we always bought at Joe's Café down the road from the school. It was the cheapest thing on the menu, and they would let us in even if we only had enough change between us to buy a couple of baskets.

'So seriously, what is up with Mr K?' Aishling had started.

'Yeah, he went off on a total rant didn't he?' Brenda had joined.

Mr K was the principal, and the rant he had gone off on was that almost nobody had signed up for the career day he had arranged for the following Saturday. So he had taken nearly twenty minutes to tell us we were all going to hell in a handbag if we didn't commit to what we were going to do for the rest of our lives.

'Give him a bit of a break,' I'd said, reaching for the dwindling fries before Tracey finished them off. 'He's new. Still has city-ideas, like the idea that people should pursue careers.'

Everyone had just blinked at me until I followed with, 'He has no idea that we all have our sights set on the high paying jobs at The Auburn Lodge.'

'Exactly!' Brenda had said.

So that had started it. How could I have known that she was serious? OK, The Auburn is a very nice hotel – very nice if you happened to be one of the V.I.P. guests being helicoptered in for the pleasure of experiencing our 'rural, rustic charm', including our garbage-can-destroying bears and lock-picking-racoons. But waiting tables for the rest of my life, panting like a dog waiting for a big tip from some guy who is loaded enough to waste his money coming to our neck of the woods, is not my idea of a career. Apparently it *was* Brenda's though, and Aishling's as well.

'He doesn't understand that we cannot possibly leave our boyfriends to attend university in a city eight hours away.' Again, the nods. 'If we did, then one of the other bimbos in town might snap him up from under our noses.' Thinking about it now, I sort of knew I was crossing a line. Brenda and Aishling had very quizzical expressions on their faces, and Brenda was turning her promise ring between her fingers. Tracey was very busy reading the menu, desperate not to catch anyone's eye.

Here was my signal to stop. But that ring on Brenda's finger bothered me. What the hell is a promise ring supposed to mean anyway? *If I could throw away my entire future for you now I would, but I will have to promise to do it when I am old enough to vote – but barely. Don't worry, I'll be all yours before I am nineteen.*

So I kept talking, and dug myself a deeper grave.

'We can't take the risk. Four years away at university, and it will be someone else living in our dream bungalows, with our increasingly fat and lazy husbands who are slowly killing themselves working in a black hole that keeps them happy with big, fat overtime cheques.'

This was a particularly personal blow to Brenda because, being in the grade above us, she was closer to this reality than the rest of us. She had been boring us for the last six months with constant references to her boyfriend, and the future she imagined. Stan was two years older than Brenda, so he was already working at the mine and saving for the bungalow. It was something Brenda was quite excited about. There wasn't a doubt in my mind that Stan and Brenda's wedding would be the first we'd all attend.

But I honestly didn't keep talking because I wanted to crush her dream, or somehow insult her. I just desperately wanted someone to *agree* with me, to wake up and think '*You're right, I can't believe we have all been happy with our stupid, ignorant little lives. We need to get out!*'

That is not what happened.

This is what happened, and I didn't see it coming.

First, there was silence. Not really the stunned kind either. More the building rage kind.

'So you think you are above us, is that it?' That was Brenda. I got the point that she was hurt, but I didn't get the 'above us' part.

'I think I kind of included myself in that group.'

'No, you didn't,' Brenda retorted. 'You think you are better than us because you have Dell. And just because your Mom is a bigshot lawyer.'

Brenda's face was bright red. Aishling had crossed her arms. Tracey's gaze was so far down she was practically look-ing behind herself.

'So let me get this straight. I think I'm better than all of you because I have a boyfriend who has every prospect of ending up to be the manager of a gas station for the rest of his life, and I have a mother who has, or should I say had, an office where she spent most of her time playing solitaire because if anyone actually needs a lawyer here, they certainly don't want it to be their neighbour.'

'That's just it, Jane!' Aishling sat closer to Brenda as she said this, the two of them a wall of opposition against me. 'You constantly put Verwood down. Just because you aren't from there.'

'I've lived there since I was six! My mother was born thirty miles away!'

'That's not the same.' Aishling was shaking her head.

'So I am constantly reminded.' I had to agree with her there. There had to be *some* reason why I couldn't seem to care about a single thing everyone else did.

We'd had fall outs before, but this one had been different. Maybe it was that we didn't need each other as much anymore. When we'd all gone to elementary school in Verwood there only *had* been us four so we kind of had to get along. In a village of 423 people, class sizes didn't leave much choice for friendship. Brenda didn't even have another girl in her year, so she'd had us by default. And at first we had clung to each other when we moved to high school, with everything new, big and overwhelming.

But now Aishling and Brenda had friends outside of our

circle. Aishling had gotten her driver's licence in the summer, and her mom let her use the car to go to Kendal on the weekends to hang out with her other friends. Brenda, of course, had Stan and his buddies.

They didn't need to repair things with me. And I had pretty much stopped giving a shit about any of it.

Tracey though, now Tracey was a bit stuck. Aishling and Brenda let her hang around with them when I wasn't there, but if she dropped off the earth tomorrow I honestly don't think they'd notice. I'm pretty sure Tracey knew that too. So I really wanted to give a shit about Tracey. At the very least I could ask her if she wanted to skip class with me. Or tell her the truth, that there wasn't a hope in hell that I would be anywhere near the school by lunchtime.

Instead I said, 'Sure, Tracey.'

And she linked my arm then and grinned as if I had just handed her a present, while the acidic guilt released in my gut caused the milk from my breakfast to curdle.

Do you ever feel like you are living your life on a tread-mill? You open your eyes in the morning and you know that it's going to be the exact same day as it was yesterday. Not one thing will have changed. And you know that you should probably just step off the bloody exercise machine, maybe even go over and try out the new stationary bike.

Only, in my case, when I look down, I realise that my treadmill is suspended over this huge chasm, and that even if I make a giant lunge for the bike, I'm probably going to fall into that black hole. I'll probably just fall forever. It will be the same as now, only darker.

I think, if I can know at all, that when I began not going to classes, it was kind of like jumping into that chasm. I thought, what the hell, it can't be worse than what is happening now, can it? The first time I just walked out of the door instead of going to class it actually felt fantastic. Like something was finally going to happen.

Only it didn't. Absolutely nothing happened. Or if it did – it had no impact on my life at all.

The bottom line is – nobody truly cares if I am there or not. Mom and Dad don't have the time or the energy to really care. And in the grand scheme of things, what is more to worry about, a daughter trying not to die, or one not doing so well in school? We all know what trumps that. So, the school is hardly going to care are they? Who is 'the school' anyway? I learned through Eva's departure that nobody was necessarily going to be there long.

It's weird though. Now that I can basically be at school whenever I want, or leave whenever I don't want to be there – it's turned into a different kind of pressure. It's up to me to decide every day whether I go or not. You'd be surprised how much effort that is. Some mornings I miss the time when I woke up whining that I really wanted to stay home, only to have Mom clap me on the back of the head and tell me that, 'no Hamilton member stayed away from work or school for something as lame as a cold'. I haven't heard that one in a couple of years now. Emma sure put a spanner in that mantra! If she had planned it, I would have congratulated her on her coup.

English was not such a bad first period to have though, especially when we were in the middle of a novel study, which we were. Ms Foster was really into her literature, and she tended to ramble on a bit when she was excited about a book. She liked the sound of her own voice and she could fill up half of the time with reading aloud to us. All the less reading to do at home.

Second period was maths, and even though I didn't love it, I had my rule – zero, two, three or five class days. So I went to maths.

Third period was family studies though, and sure, it was an easy class, but we were doing some sort of project where we had to work in groups. I'd missed too many classes to really follow it; something about planning and budgeting for a household. My group were all terribly keen and taking the project to a whole new level, with elaborate plans of 'our house' and how they were going to decorate it for free.

When I did go to the class, they all kind of sighed, so it was better not to go at all. I couldn't even pretend to be excited about decorating some virtual house, and even though I know they all resented that I was going to end up sharing their good grade, while doing absolutely nothing to contribute, I also knew they were happier if I wasn't there to remind them of that fact.

So I walked into town instead, which has its own pitfalls. What is it about those of us between the ages of thirteen and seventeen that threatens the retail industry so much? I haven't been able to walk into a store for more than two years without feeling like I should hold my hands in the air just so there's no question about my shoplifting intentions. And I mean really, in a town the size of Kendal, am I honestly going to try to fleece people? I'm not stupid. In the winter, when all of the tourists have left, there can't be more than ten customers a day. Ten customers, minus three who are relatives, three who are Grannies, equals a one in four chance that I would be blamed for any discrepancy in stock at the end of the day. No way would I chance it, even if I felt like lifting something, which I generally do not.

All I am looking for in town is somewhere to get out of the weather once in a while. Did I mention that it's November and absolutely freezing? There hasn't been any snow, but that is only because it's too bloody cold to snow. So it isn't even pretty and cold. Just cold.

What I usually do when the temperature reaches the requiring-mittens-to-avoid-losing-fingers-to-frostbite stage is to do some intense browsing, for very short periods of time, in as many stores as it takes to eat up the time I have to kill. Twenty stores, or there-about, at ten minutes per store, equals two hundred minutes at a push. I can tell you what is in any store in town. I could open a business as a personal shopper in a snap.

Only I hate shopping. I never buy anything. Not that I could even if I wanted to. I believe it's about nineteen months since Mom and Dad completely stopped supplying me with regular, predictable chore money. You know, the kind you can count on every Saturday, even if it's only a few bob? I'm not sure if the chore money stopped because (a) I stopped doing chores at all or (b) they could no longer afford it with Mom not working at all now or (c) which is most likely — they stopped remembering that they wanted to teach their daughters 'the value of money' and 'how to manage your own finances'.

We used to have lengthy discussions about this sort of thing. If I remember correctly, most of the conversations went along the line of Emma smiling sweetly, and me arguing every point Mom and Dad said. Something like:

'Dad, can I have some money to buy Tracey a present for her birthday?'

'That really isn't my expense, Jane. That's what your chore

money is for,' Dad replied.

'But her birthday party is on Friday, and I don't get my chore money until Saturday,' I protested.

'Again, not my fault. You need to plan for these things. You mean you don't have one cent saved?' He knew the answer to that was no, of course.

'I have seventy-nine dollars,' Emma had quipped from her corner of the breakfast table.

'Well good for you, Miss Saver-of-the-Year.' Emma had a way of saying the worst things at the worst time. To be fair, she didn't mean to make me look bad; she just instinctively could not pass up an opportunity to look good, and by comparison, I always provided the perfect backdrop for that.

'Jane, there's no need for snarkiness here.'

'Well, it's super easy to not spend any money when you spend every day in some sort of rehearsal – which is totally paid for by your parents I might add. Whereas myself, I have a social life and it takes money to have one of those.'

I'd *had* a social life. I guess I didn't need money anymore without one. It was just one more thing that I couldn't seem to care about anymore. It all seemed too monotonous to care about. The conversations never went anywhere. It was the same thing over and over. Talk about who was with who, who wanted to be with who, what so and so had done at the last party, what shoes were so cool, what band was so cool. I kind of hated everyone, except maybe Dell, but then it's difficult to hate someone who generally doesn't talk.

Everything that came out of anyone's mouth anymore seemed utterly meaningless. I watched their mouths move. The words came out with not one bit of effort. Their expressions flickered, bright sparks that came and went; they cared about what they said, how they felt. Those words started out vibrant and light, but by the time they got to my ears, they were flat and heavy. I had a difficult time believing that the person uttering them even believed them. Could people really be as happy as they seemed? Really?

I longed to feel that happiness. I wanted to believe them, to feel what they seemed to. I just couldn't.

That's another reason, maybe, that I had a hard time staying in school for too many hours at a time. All of that bubbly joy sticking to me as I passed people in the halls made me start to feel kind of itchy. An itch that I couldn't find to scratch. If I didn't get away from it I felt I might end up in a corner screaming. That couldn't be good.

So here I was walking the streets of the big town of Kendal again, reading the sandwich boards outside shops, as if there would be something new written on them, as if I were doing a little early Christmas shopping. Some of the signs were already flat on their faces, blown over by the gusts of wind that punched down the street every once in a while. I stopped to put the sports shop sign right, but the next one – for the novelty shop – I left because my mittens were at home instead of in my jacket pocket where they should be, and my fingers were already losing feeling. Besides, the sports shop sign had hit the ground again with a thud as soon as I walked away from it.

I was having a harder time deciding which shop I could go into for a few minutes because there were hardly any people around. It was difficult to appear inconspicuous when you were the only one in a store. I was just walking past 'the granola café', as it was nicknamed, when the door slammed open. Bad timing; it had just been hit by a gust. The guy coming through the door couldn't do much about it because he had his own sandwich board in his hands – and I seemed to be exactly in the spot he wanted to put it.

'Hmmm.' He put the sign down, and instead of closing the door like a normal human being would, he just stood there looking at me. Like I was a painting or something. In the wind, with his heavy wooden sign leaning on him, with the door still wide open. I wondered what he was even doing holding that sign instead of being in school. Unless he looked young for his age. Maybe it was the spelt bread that those types had to eat.

It wasn't like the street was crowded and I could just carry on. This guy was STARING at me, and you know when someone does something weird and you think that you need to do something, respond in some way, but your brain hasn't figured out what the correct response is? It was like that.

Finally, after tons of seconds went by and he was still staring at me, my brain came up with that response. It wasn't perhaps the cleverest of responses mind you.

'And?' I said.

'I didn't know the universe would respond so promptly.'

'Excuse me?' The picture was getting clearer. This guy was obviously off-his-rocker stoned. A little early for it, but he fit the profile alright. Kind of. Not really. Well, he was outside of the right shop anyway.

Let me explain about where I live. There are two kinds of people: you are either 'an earth ravager' or you are 'an earth saver'. That sounds kind of extreme, and it is. You also can't really do much about which camp you are in if you are under the age of say eighteen. It all depends on what your parents do. If you are a logging or a mining family, then you are 'an earth ravager'. Too bad for you if you are interested in saving the rain forest. If, on the other hand, you had the weird luck of being born into one of the communes (probably literally there, in a pond, with a whale sound track in the background) then you are 'an earth saver'. Again, if you fancy getting yourself a souped-up car, and a nice house, paid for by a fat mine paycheque, well you better not voice that goal to your family. Now I'm not saying that I am a climate-change denying, death-to-the-left-wing fanatics because my dad happens to work for the mine. I'm not. I'm actually pretty anti-corporation of any kind. Maybe Brenda is right, and I haven't embraced my 'earth ravaging' community values because my dad isn't your typical miner. He's actually an artist-turned-miner to pay the bills.

Somehow I highly doubt there's a whole lot of differ-ence between the two camps though. We are all stuck in this shithole. The hippies are stuck because most of them are descended from draft dodgers – a bunch of Americans who avoided getting sent to some war – by hiding out in Canada instead; maybe they can't even get passports! The loggers and miners are stuck because, let's be honest, have you ever talked to a logger who suddenly changed career and became, say, a teacher, who could get a job anywhere they wanted? Not going to happen.

And us kids? We just don't meet anyone from the other camp. Really, really we don't. There's even the hippie school for the hippies. I think they do a lot of baking and making bad clay coffee cups. At least that's what I know of the school from the spring market. Our school sells raffle tickets for all of the consumer goods donated by business. You get the picture.

The guy standing in front of me was obviously from the baking/pottery side of things. He literally had the sign in front of him stating it: 'From the Good Earth', which was the name of the café. Plus, he had on one of those Guatemalan stripy shirts, with a pair of Birkenstock sandals, in November.

But instead of the usual dreadlocks or stringy ponytail, he had massive hair. Massive, disco-seventies, afro hair. It just didn't match his outfit. Although, what did I know? I mean, it's not like there are very many people who are black around Kendal at all. But then I remembered the picture of Bob Marley, and of course, of all hippies, one who is black *should* have dreadlocks.

As interesting as all of this was, in a rather uncomfortable sort of way, I was beginning to freeze. And this weirdo just stood there. But then another gust of wind nearly took the sign sideways out of his hands and woke him up.

'You need to come inside,' he said, propping the sign up against the brick wall, where it was obviously going to fall with the next gust.

'I don't need to do anything,' I protested, but he had already linked my elbow with his and was pulling me in the door.

'Yes you do. You just don't know it yet.'

Who did this guy think he was? Cocky, arrogant fucker. Besides, all I had in my pocket was a few small coins. I couldn't even buy a hot chocolate – if there were such a thing here. It was probably hot carob at twice the price.

'Here.' He had guided me over to a table covered in books and binders. He even had to clear a pile off one chair so that he had a place to put me. And then he didn't so much offer me the chair as push me into it. I may have been more concerned about practically being kidnapped except that it wasn't just us in the café. There was a woman behind the counter who didn't seem fazed by our windy entrance; she was flipping through a newspaper and barely glanced up.

'You might close the door behind you, Farley,' she said, turning another page. This he did, before sitting opposite to me, grinning widely.

'She can't be serious. Your name isn't really Farley, is it?'

'What's wrong with that?'

'As in Farley Mowatt? The guy who wrote all of those books about owls and wolves that they made us read in elementary?'

'Obviously without the Mowatt,' he said, still grinning. 'You didn't think he was the only Farley in the world did you?'

'It's not something I spend a lot of time contemplating, Farley.' Extra emphasis on the Farley. Usually I try to temper my sarcasm, especially after the debacle with Brenda and Aishling, but this guy seemed to invite it.

'So, what *do* you spend time contemplating?' As if we *knew* each other; as if, naturally, I wanted to share that with him.

'Well, Farley, I was contemplating leaving now.'

'Can't,' he stated. 'You're meant to be here.'

'What, did the stars tell you this?' I didn't seem to be able to rattle Farley. And it didn't seem like this was any strange pick-up scenario. I wasn't sure what it was.

'Not strictly speaking the stars, but I suppose they are a part of it.' He wouldn't stop grinning like a bloody Cheshire cat.

'Sorry to disappoint you, Farley, but I think you have hooked yourself to the wrong star.' It was just about time to leave I thought, before he started trying to sell me some kind of hippie book that was somehow going to transform my life. Fat chance of that happening.

'No, serendipity tells me I haven't.'

'And what is that supposed to mean?'

'I was just saying to Kaitlin – that's Kaitlin by the way.' He pointed to the woman behind the counter, who gave a wave, without looking up from her magazine. 'I was just saying that the weather today reminded me of the opening scene in Mary Poppins, where the wind is blowing and you know someone magical is going to come along. And then you did.'

'Farley, it's not even noon. There's a whole day for this "someone magical" to actually come along – if you think that is going to make your day.' I didn't even know this guy, but somehow his optimism bothered me.

'Oh, you've already made my day.'

'Good. Then I can go now.' I stood up.

'So what is your name?' Farley asked, as I slung my backpack over my shoulder and prepared to go back into the wind.

'You mean the stars didn't tell you that?'

'Nope.' That infuriating grin did not waver.

'It's Jane. Plain Jane. No magic here.' And strangely, saying that made my eyes prickle, which made me feel not just annoyed, but angry. I didn't need some weirdo who wouldn't stop smiling to tell me there was some sort of destiny at work in his life. He was pretty stupid if he thought there was, and he could go off and believe what he liked — but he'd have to find another random stranger to pretend with.

I stomped to the door, turning just long enough to say, 'See. Quite capable of leaving.'

'For now,' and he waved as I slammed the door shut.

As soon as I was out of the door, I wanted to be back in, which was weird because I was still angry. Maybe feeling anger was better than feeling nothing.

Now, with the anger fading, all I was feeling was cold. And I still had to waste a couple of hours. A woman across the road got out of her car, racing the wind to the convenience store, so I headed there. At least I wouldn't be the only one in there. Maybe I could get away with looking through magazines, pretending I gave a shit about whoever the current celebrity divorcing some other celebrity was.

It wasn't until I was just about to follow the woman in that I remembered that I didn't like coming in this shop. The little bell that tinkled when she opened the door reminded me of the times I used to stop here to pick up the newspaper for Grandad. He had read a ton of them, but whichever one I had bought him, using my own money usually, it had somehow always been the wrong one. *'Nothing but gossip. Left-wing rhetoric. It's not Sunday – The Globe saves all the best articles for then.'* Even stepping in the door made me feel like I was going to disappoint him, though it was too late for that.

It was too cold to indulge my avoidance of Grandad memories by walking out though, so I pushed those thoughts away, and concentrated on doing my best casual saunter instead. So much for picking a store that had more than me as the potential customer though. The woman I'd followed in didn't look like she was going to take her time. She went straight to the dairy fridge and then headed to the counter with her milk.

I positioned myself to be ignored, keeping most of me between the magazine shelf and the shelf lined with pasta sauces, out of the line of sight of the man at the till.

'It's a cold one,' he said as he rang up the woman's milk.

'It can blow all it wants as long as the snow stays away,' I heard her say. 'You can keep the change. Where's your jar for that little girl in Verwood?'

'Here, put it in the SPCA box. The jar is full and nobody has stopped by to empty it in a while. I was thinking maybe she didn't make it, poor thing. Haven't heard anything for ages.'

'If it was one of my kids, I don't know how I'd go on at all. They say it's the worst thing that can happen, losing a child.'

The page in the magazine I was trying to read went out of focus I was staring at it so hard. It felt like I couldn't move, like I wasn't in control of my body. I wanted to feel upset, or angry, but I didn't. Not even five minutes ago I had been irate at a guy I didn't even know, but now I felt nothing about someone talking about my sister as if she were dead.

This was the worst bit, that sometimes I felt like I should feel something more about the whole thing with Emma, but mostly I couldn't. There was just this numb sort of hole where there used to be a confusion of love and resentment and pride and all those sorts of sister-emotions. Now, when that hole filled up with anything, it was always with pure toxic feelings – like dread, or fear.

I may have continued to just stand there, searching for a feeling, but as soon as the woman left, the man called to me.

'Can I help you with anything?'

Putting the magazine down, I walked to the counter, hoping I had enough in my pocket to buy something – any-thing. I found the chips Emma likes on the rack and put them on the counter before fishing in my pocket for change.

'She's still kicking it,' I said.

'Sorry?'

'Emma. Her name is Emma, and she is still alive.'

'Oh, that's good news indeed. She is such a sweet little thing; I hope she beats this bastard cancer.'

'Oh, don't you worry. There's sure to be another tragic case coming up soon for everyone to gossip about.' I slid the change onto the counter. I was pretty sure it wasn't enough, but he didn't even check it before putting it in the till.

'Oh, well…' he stumbled on the words, but I saved him the effort by leaving before he could think of something appropriate to say to me. I knew how it was. The concept of tragedy is so much more pleasant than the actual reality of it.

Sometimes I use the time on the bus to do a little homework. I guess spending so much time on a bus is my saving grace; it's what has made it possible for me to maintain my current status, a solid C average, while attending so few classes. Maybe that just speaks to our poor educational system – that I can be nearly absent for three years and still get by.

Mostly though, I open a book and leave it there on my lap while I lean my head against the window pane instead. The scenes passing are pretty familiar at this point. Trees, trees,

trees, a house, trees, trees, a little farm, trees, a glimpse of a deer.

There are little stories if you notice the details though. At one house – a big white dog and a woman throwing sticks for it on nice days has given way to tricycles and plastic peddle cars, the dog only seen as a blur of white fur behind the fence now. At another – a ramp connecting the front door to the drive appeared over a week of construction. I've seen the old man living there pushing his wife down that ramp more than once since. The bus never slows enough for me to see their expressions, but I make them up in doodles I add to the margins of my copy books. Sometimes both are very sad. In others her expression is vacant and mindless, his determination etched in every deep line marching across his face.

I doodle roads that lead from dark pine forests to wide open, manicured parks with fountains and lakes where little boys sail toy boats. I doodle monsters with open mouths that swallow houses and cars. Mostly people though. Mostly faces with a million different expressions.

I don't know when these doodles started. I don't remember drawing when I was younger. Not that I would call what I do now drawing. It's just this mindless place I go to, that results in bits of pictures and patterns. Sometimes I cover them with criss-crossed lines of obscurity when they're done. Occasionally I like the scribbles though and so I tear the pages out and stuff them in the back pocket of my back-pack, behind my laptop. I don't know why. I'm never going to take them out again. The bag is beginning to bulge with the crumpled papers.

You would think that I would feel comfortable in the hospi-tal by now. I've spent a good chunk of my memorable teen years there. I don't though. Every single time I get off the bus and start to walk toward it my body begins to tense. It doesn't help that the hospital is the most imposing building in the whole town. It isn't exactly like there are any other tall buildings in town – so the four stories and one block of space it takes up make it kind of stand out. It's the way it seems to stare me down as I walk toward it, leaning toward me the closer I get, almost like it disapproves of me and would like to swallow me up like a pile of bricks, that makes me feel on edge.

I don't let it beat me though. I can't. I've a little sister inside, and I won't let the hospital keep her.

Emma, however, seems completely oblivious to being in the belly of a monster. She is perfectly at home, even when the drugs are stealing every bit of colour from her body or turning her insides out. Which wasn't the case today, thank god.

Today Emma was smiling. And the bloody DVD player was firmly shut. It was a good day.

'What's up, Ems?' I greeted, throwing her the bag of ketchup chips I still had in my pocket. For some reason, ketchup chips are the one thing she can always eat, no matter how sick she is. 'What has your frown turned upside down?'

That was from this picture book Mom used to read to us when we were little. It had all of these cartoons where the picture changed completely if you turned the book the other way around. That part was pretty cool, but we both used to hate the stupid story that went with it. It wasn't even a story; it was some unimaginative adult's idea of teaching kids about emotions. At some point lines from that book had become a code for how we know how each other is feeling. Me and Emma need that kind of system. We don't do emotional stuff well.

'A break from the Adriamycin,' she declared, like I knew what that meant. Emma and Mom speak 'cancereze' fluently. Dad, he gets by, asking for a bit of translation every now and then. Me? I am a definite foreigner. Nobody ever offered to teach me, but I never volunteered myself for lessons either. The problem is, so many conversations in the hospital are conducted in this foreign language. It's better when Emma is at home; everyone starts to speak English again. I've given up counting on those spells to last, though – they never do.

'Is that a good thing?' I wasn't entirely being sarcastic. In my limited, foreign understanding, the times when Emma was most sick, were the times just before she started to get better. 'I thought you were down for another week of that?'

'Yep. I was.'

'So, what, they just decided the puking was a sign to stop?' It had never been a sign before. In my estimation, the goal had always been to kill off every bit of Emma, before bringing her back from the brink.

'I don't know.' Emma shrugged, but the space between where her eyebrows should have been gave her worry away. Since she was little, when she was scared or unsure, Emma's eyebrows would come so close together it would look like she had a uni-brow. It used to happen to her all of the time on the way to dance performances. I'd glance over at her, in the back seat beside me, where she would be sitting, completely still, giving nothing of her nervousness away besides her eyebrow thing. It wasn't so obvious now that she had lost her dark brown eyebrows.

'But it is a good thing,' I stated, even though we both knew it probably wasn't. When plans changed, it always meant something was wrong. Emma would follow my lead though. Mostly it's as if Emma has never moved past being ten. She still believes anything I tell her. 'Any day I can play Monopoly with you instead of holding a puke container is a good day.'

Sure enough, she smiled again and I got the board out

of the cupboard. Emma loves Monopoly, even though she almost always loses. Sometimes I hate that she is so easy to please. It makes me so difficult by comparison. I'd always sort of hoped she'd grow into a rebellious teen. It happens doesn't it? The nicest, most compliant kids decide one day that they have had enough of that and suddenly they're the ones having house wrecker parties and doing community time for shop lifting.

Instead, she got to be a perpetual child and I had to keep being the rebellious one for both of us. And it wasn't even fun anymore. How do you rebel when nobody cares? How do you rebel when you no longer care yourself?

We just had the board set up when a doctor came in. That always happens. I don't know how Emma even manages to have a pee some days without being interrupted. Mostly it's the nurses at random times though; doctors tend to keep to the schedule of morning rounds.

'Thought I'd check on you before I put my head down for a while,' he said. His bright blue scrubs labelled him as an intern. Not that anyone would mistake him for anything more qualified anyway. He looked like he was about twelve. A cute twelve, but still twelve, and unlikely to know anything about treating a case as complicated as my sister's.

'Hi, I'm Dr Jonathan,' he introduced himself to me, sticking out his hand for a handshake. I didn't take it.

'Do they not let you blue-coats use your last names?'

'Um, no. There aren't any rules to it.' I'd thrown him, but he recovered. 'The coats and the gear are enough to make lots of kids scared, without dealing with a surname as well.'

'Which is?' I persisted.

'Does it matter?'

'Most definitely.' I couldn't let it go now.

'Ballerini. It's Italian.'

Emma and I both started to laugh. How perfect was that?

'And there is that,' he sighed, smiling though. 'Kind of difficult to be taken seriously once the name is out there.'

'That's not true,' Emma said. 'This doctor knows his stuff, Jane. He was the only one who knew exactly what to do for my rash. I just had to put some garlic on it.' She held up her arm, showing me her elbows that had been red and raw for weeks, but that now looked considerably better.

'Technically it's the ajoene in garlic that helps,' Dr Jonathan said, before putting his finger to his mouth. 'Shhh. Herbal remedies are not exactly popular around here. They're practically contraband for us blue-coats.'

'But it worked,' Emma protested.

'Working, and being funded by the pharmaceuticals is an entirely different thing,' he said.

'Thanks for checking me. I'm a ton better.' She was. I knew it from the way I felt like giving her a shove for her sickening sweetness.

By the time Mom came back I had three complete sets

of property, and Emma had a lot of different properties that were going to earn her nothing. Mom immediately picked up Emma's chart, even though she had only been gone less than an hour and could have asked us if someone had been around.

'Mom, there are nurses employed for that you know,' I said. 'It's kind of why Emma is here.'

'It's an agency nurse today,' she said absently. She looked wrecked.

'Listen, I could stay here tonight. You could go home.' I wasn't sure if I hoped she would accept or reject my offer. I pretty much knew what the response would be though.

'I can stay by myself,' Emma said.

'Don't be ridiculous.' She meant that for both of us. She had taken on Emma's illness with the same stubborn obsessiveness she previously had for her law business. We all knew there was not a chance she would let me take her place or let Emma stay on her own at this stage in Emma's treatment. Especially if it wasn't one of the regular nurses on.

I don't know why, but for once I wanted to ask Mom to come home, to leave Emma for one night and to come home. Maybe it was the weird morning that had jogged my brain out of autopilot, where I no longer hoped for anything to change. Was one trip home, just her and me in the car, too much to ask for?

Now that I had thought it, I wanted that, even though it

couldn't happen. I wanted her to ask me about my day, and I could tell her about the disco-haired boy – only changing the context of how I had met him of course, to avoid questions of why I was wandering the streets of Kendal. I wanted her to confide in me, to tell me why Emma was off the drug that was the one that was going to work this time.

It was on the tip of my tongue to say *Mom, Emma is much better today – just for once, can you come home with me?*

Before I could ever hope to say something that foreign for us both though, she spoke the words that were much more familiar.

'You better get going, Jane.' She fished around in her handbag and came out with a twenty dollar note. 'Pick up some of those burritos Dad likes on the way home. The fridge must be almost empty.'

That's what hope got me; thinking something didn't make it happen. The most I could hope to get from Mom was burritos that would be stone cold by the time I got them home. She hardly even looked at me as she resumed her usual place in the chair beside Emma, kicking off her shoes so she could curl her feet under her, like a cat getting comfortable in a familiar chair. I'd never seen her sit like that at home.

Emma was already handing Mom my Monopoly money. I meant nothing here.

'I don't think I'm going to play with you anymore,

Emma.' Resentment rose in my throat, spilling out with my words. 'You're a crap player; it gets so boring.' And suddenly I was on sure ground again, hearing Mom's sigh, full of exasperation, and Emma hunching her shoulders, though only I would notice it, draped as she still was in my too-large hoodie.

Dell ate the cold burritos as we watched reality show reruns on T.V. I wasn't hungry.

Dad said he had already eaten when I offered to make him soup again. I doubted that, but I didn't argue. I still wasn't hungry.

I woke up in the dark, with my shoes and jeans still on. I couldn't remember when I had fallen asleep. I hadn't even taken out my text books, or opened my laptop. I'm not sure what I was even doing before I fell asleep. Just looking at the ceiling I guess. When Dell and I first got together I remember I had spent a lot of time lying on my bed remembering every bit of his profile, savouring in the thrill that he had noticed me, liked me, kissed me.

I didn't do that anymore. I couldn't remember when I had last had a feeling I cared about. There weren't any more thoughts worth thinking about either.

I felt around for a while before I found my phone to check the time. It was only 4am, but I was awake now. I was cold, but I didn't get under the covers to warm up. I wanted to feel the cold — it was something wasn't it? I folded my arms over my chest, Snow White or Dracula-style, and looked up into the dark. What would happen if I just stayed in this position and refused to move? Refused to speak. Isn't that what women did in the Victorian times, just took to the bed and refused to get out? It seemed to me a reasonable thing to do. If your life was shit and not likely to ever improve, why not just stop getting on with it?

I closed my eyes and concentrated on the patterns playing against my eyelids, pulses of white light that reminded me of stars. Out there somewhere other people were fully alive. I could stay here and not try to be one of them anymore. It would be easier without me in their faces to remind them what half dead looked like.

The problem with my apathy is that I can never seem to sink right into it. There are all of these annoying spider webs covering my pit of despair that stop me from descending any more than half-way. So two hours later I woke up under my duvet and without the will to spend the day in bed. Let's be real here, my parents hardly needed two kids stuck in bed.

When I got on the bus and Tracey was turned in her seat, chatting with Aishling and Brenda in the seat behind her, I took a breath, determined not to say anything insulting. Tracey flashed me a nervous smile, swinging her legs out so that I could slide in beside her, giving me the window because she knew I preferred it. Then she glanced at the others, who kept decidedly neutral expressions.

I had interrupted a conversation and they tried to find a way back into it tentatively, warily. I had ruined too many conversations in the past.

'So, Tracey, you were telling us what you were going to wear to the disco,' Aishling said.

'Well …' Again Tracey looked at me before proceeding. I felt like saying, '*It's okay, you don't need my approval to talk about your wardrobe selection for a stupid school dance.*' I didn't say that though; I just smiled. 'Okay, so I have a blue dress that is pretty casual, but I think it might be way too short. And, can I get away with heels if it's casual? Because I have these amazing new shoes.'

'Oh, I don't think Aaron would mind that, do you Aishling?' said Brenda.

Tracey went red. She had been hoping to get together with this Aaron since last spring. She doesn't say it often, but we know it from how she lights up like a Christmas tree every time we say his name.

Unfortunately, it's totally wishful thinking. Though she is absolutely beautiful, somehow the guys just don't flock to her at all. I think she scares them. See, as soon as there are any males in sight who could possibly be boyfriend material it's as if Tracey loses the ability to speak at all. *I* know that is because she is so nervous that her brain freezes, but I don't think they do. It's not like any of the guys we know are exactly great conversationalists, but any guy that tries to move in on her ends up giving up because they don't know what to do with her utter silence. Alcohol can't even help her, because with more than one beer she is in the bathroom praying to the porcelain god. She is terrified to try any drugs given the effect booze has on her.

'What about you?' Tracey turned to me. 'Will you come?'

I didn't say anything.

'Dell can meet us after with Stan if he wants. You won't be the only one without your second half.'

I didn't even know when the disco was on. Was it this Friday? Next? I couldn't remember when I had last been to one. It wasn't that Dell would care if I went either. To him, dances, school or otherwise, were girl's territory; he didn't dance — ever.

I used him as an excuse to avoid going out anyway, most of the time. He was convenient that way. I couldn't stomach putting on makeup, doing my hair, finding something to wear. I just couldn't seem to care.

'Dell and I are … we're,' I searched for a plausible excuse. 'He said he has a surprise for my birthday.' I hoped the dance was this weekend. I had only just remembered that I had a birthday coming. Sixteen. Sweet sixteen.

'I thought you were never going to mention your birthday!' Tracey exclaimed. 'That sounds really amazing! Maybe Dell's taking you for a romantic dinner. Maybe his dad is away for the night. If not, I can get you the keys to our cabin.' In Tracey's world, every girl is just waiting for a knight in shining armour to rush her off into the romantic ever after. I'm sure she thinks having sex with the first guy who doesn't run away from her will be her gateway to Nirvana. I wasn't going to burst that bubble.

'Mm hmm.' I hoped that nonspecific mumbling would shift the focus off me before I said something I regretted. I was trying to remember what the date was. Hard to believe I had forgotten my own birthday. I guess the topic hadn't come up at home. Emma hadn't exactly been well, even for the skewed definition of well that seemed to apply to her lately.

'Anyway.' Brenda flashed me a smile that I was sure meant *Enough about Jane.* 'Kayla didn't specifically say we were invited, but she did tell me her parents are away that night and people are going over to hers after the disco. I'd say we could show up there.'

'And Stan can get us some beer!' Aishling proclaimed.

PLAIN JANE

This was my life. I pretended to be tired, so I could lean my head on the frozen glass window pane. I listened with my eyes closed. They were so excited, genuinely. This dance, and the promise of a party, was everything. I wanted so badly to feel that excitement. I concentrated on that spot in my stomach where I knew I should feel it. I know there was a time when I would have buzzed, literally, with the anticipation of a house party, a disco, the promise of all sorts of debauchery and gossip-inducing happenings.

I just couldn't find that feeling now. And without the feeling – well, it just seemed like a meaningless thing to be excited about. Nothing would be different from any other party I had ever attended. I would drink as fast as I could, until everything began to spin. Tracey would cling to me, hopeful and terrified that tonight would be the night she found love. Some big guy would break something. Two girls would argue over something. The evening would progress to groups of girls jumping up and down to bad house music. Couples would retreat to corners and rooms, and when I needed the toilet I would come across them awkwardly in my search for a bathroom that didn't have a half hour queue to it. Finally, the police would come, or neighbours, or worse yet the parents themselves. Everyone would complain and try to grab their beer in retreat, while secretly loving the drama of it all.

I didn't need to go. It wouldn't be any different from any

66

other night. Still, I wished I did want to go, that I could forget that it would be the same as every other night. Why was everyone else able to do that? Why couldn't I?

When I was sure the girls had forgotten I was there, I opened my eyes again. It was still dark – and freezing because the windows never shut properly. I couldn't see anything out of the window, but the frost had made patterns in its attempt to cover the pane and I tried to lose myself in the intricate twists. I traced the tendrils with my fingernail, catching the curls of ice that fell away, wishing the cold would hurt before melting.

English, History, PE.

Take the bus to Red River.

Sit in the corner for an hour while Mom and Emma laugh, watching a sitcom that I don't even know, and isn't one bit funny.

Get soaked walking through sleet to catch the bus back home.

Watch Dell play some war game for two hours. Count the words he says to me: twenty-six.

Go home and wake Dad up. Put his plate, with its half-eaten sandwich on the pile of dishes in the kitchen.

Get into bed still wearing my jeans and hoodie. Open my laptop, but fall asleep before writing even one sentence of my English assignment.

Wash, rinse, repeat.

You know those mornings when you wake up, and maybe the sun is shining, or you had a great dream, or you think it's Friday or then suddenly remember that it's Saturday? And you think it might be kind of a good day? I woke up with that feeling, even though it was still dark out and definitely not Saturday. Something just felt … different. I'd even heard Mom come in the door late the night before. Of course she would come home. It was my birthday today.

So here is my confession. I may be a pretty cynical bitch about most things, most of the time, but birthdays are different. I've always loved my birthday. My whole family loves birthdays. Even my practical, no nonsense mother loves birthdays. We have whole-day rituals for them, starting with breakfast in bed for the birthday-celebrator and ending with one of Mom's cakes – which never turn out to look like the picture she is going for, but always taste delicious.

Birthdays, the actual day, have always been for just our family. Emma or I might have a sleepover with friends, or a party, on another day, but never on our real birthday. The actual day is reserved for pampering by our foursome.

We scheme about birthdays. It's never about big, flashy gifts, or fancy meals — it's about showing that you have listened the whole year through to what matters. Like the year that Dad carved me a family of penguins because I had been obsessed with the *March of the Penguins* movie for months. Emma and I even declared a temporary truce on these days. Or — I did in any case, which meant she didn't have to defend herself.

I wasn't expecting the whole ritual this year of course. Everything was put on hold when Emma was in the hospital. That was understandable. But still.

I didn't even know what I might get for a present this year. I hadn't dropped any hints at all, having pretty much forgotten that my birthday was coming. Sixteen was kind of a big one though.

It was hard not to be at least a little excited. It had been a long time since I'd felt like there was anything worth getting excited about. I ran down the stairs like I was five. And that is not like me — not in the morning. Even before life became an endurance test I did not like mornings.

For the briefest moment I thought maybe Mom had brought Emma home too. That would be the best present. Maybe we could all just stay home, eat pizza and watch a few movies together.

She hadn't though.

Mom hadn't even bothered to stay herself until I woke up. Her car was gone. So was Dad's truck; he was working another double shift. It was just me, and it wasn't even light yet. Another dark school morning.

I looked into every room just in case. Maybe there was a big present lurking somewhere. With every new door I opened though, I knew there wasn't. There wasn't even a card, or a note.

There must have been an important reason for Mom to have left Emma overnight, even if she had left before dawn to go back again. The reason wasn't my birthday though.

I opened every last door, even the closets – just in case.

The worst part about there being nothing was that I understood it. I got it that nobody would remember that I was sixteen today. *I* had barely remembered.

It wasn't even like I really cared about the present. Not much anyway. I just wanted the day to be different, not the same as every other day. If it couldn't be a good day, then I wanted it to be a horrible day. I wanted to feel something – anger, or sadness, anything at all.

But I didn't. I just felt heavy and tired and I didn't want to face another day. Not one more day.

I thought about staying home. That promised too many hours in the day to face alone though. Daytime television had a way of making the hours stretch out even longer. Maybe if

Dell wasn't working I'd have stayed in Verwood, but he was. If I didn't get on the school bus I would be stuck in the village even if I changed my mind about not going to school.

So I went.

Tracey was watching out for me. Brenda and Aishling were hunched down in their seat, knees against the seat in front of them, talking about god knows what boring thing, but Tracey had her eyes to the front, waiting for me to come up the steps at my stop. She smiled her shy half-smile when she saw me and as soon as I sat down beside her she slipped a little box into my pocket.

'It's not much,' she said, before the other two popped up from behind the seat, and they all embarrassed me by singing Happy Birthday as loudly as they could.

'Cupcakes. I made them last night,' Aishling announced, opening the lid on a cookie tin, revealing multi-coloured cakes, each with a candy '16' in the middle. She smiled before passing the tin to me. 'First one to the birthday girl.'

I wanted to smash all of the horrible thoughts I'd had about the three. Horrible, awful thoughts, even about Tracey, and god, how could anyone hate Tracey?

'I know you have plans with Dell for Friday night, but how about we stay in town after school today?' Tracey was looking at me like my answer would make or break her week. How could she continue being so good to me? 'My mom will even come to pick us up later on, if you want?'

I tried to want to do this. For Tracey. I couldn't remember when we had properly hung out together. It had been weeks ago. What did we even do? What did we talk about? I couldn't remember and the thought of walking the streets of Kendal for fun just made me feel tired and cold. The seconds were ticking and Tracey was still looking expectantly at me.

'Yeah, well, I'll have to check with Mom first,' I said. 'Sometimes she needs a break, and Emma isn't so, well she's okay … but … it's just a long time she's been in hospital.'

'Yeah, I know how it is.' Tracey nodded ardently, but she didn't know how it was at all. Even mentioning Emma was enough to quiet everyone for a while though.

The bus slowed as we neared town. It was early still and there weren't many cars on the road. Not that there were many cars on the road in the middle of the day either. Not in November. A nothing month. No summer tourists, no holidays, no sun and no snow yet to lure the ski and snowboard types.

The bus turned onto Main Street and we passed the park. Until a month ago it had been filled with tents and signs. Groups of dreadlocked boys and flowing-skirted girls had sat around with guitars, openly smoking weed and occasionally shouting slogans all summer.

Slowly, the tents had been disappearing; it seems even hippies didn't have the energy to care about anything in November. Today, all the tents were gone. All that was left was one broken one, minus the poles, that had been blown into the fence, and was flapping goodbye.

'I wonder if they won,' I said. I had meant to think this thought; the words slipped out before I could stop them.

'What was it even about?' Brenda quipped.

'They're always about the same thing – stopping jobs,' said Aishling. I swear I'd heard the exact same words from her dad.

'They wanted a sanctuary for the grizzly bears,' I said. It didn't seem like such an unreasonable thing.

'Why would they care?' said Brenda. 'Notice that their tent city was in downtown Kendal – not up in the alpine with the bears?'

'I'd say they were all from Vancouver anyway. Probably just getting away from the parents and smoking loads of dope,' agreed Aishling, as if she didn't aspire to the same goal every weekend.

I wondered if Farley had been part of that group. Maybe he had gone home now. That was probably a good thing.

'I don't know,' I said, but I said it quietly for once, and I kept my next thoughts to myself. *'At least they have something besides themselves to care about. At least they were fighting for something that mattered to them, and not just filling the days.'*

First period was history. I hadn't read the chapter that I was supposed to have read for homework. That turned out to be okay though, because we were just watching a film. We were on World War II and our teacher must have loved this topic because there has to be a million movies and documentaries about the Second World War – all curriculum approved it seems. Easy days for her. Happy Birthday to me too.

The movie today wasn't about the most cheery of themes though, even for a world war. We could have watched something with lots of plane battles, and things to cheer for. Instead, we were watching *Schindler's List*, which was about the holocaust, and so didn't promise one thing to cheer about. I think the teacher picked it because it's so long. It was going to take up three classes – a reward for having finished everything we had to cover before our term exam the following week. If I'd had known it was just a movie, I would have skipped the class.

I guess if you were in the mood for getting depressed it would be a good movie. I was not really in the mood for getting any more depressed though. All it did was remind me how meaningless my life was, and I didn't exactly need any reminders for that either.

The guy in it was saving thousands of people. *Thousands.* Even though we didn't get too far into it before the bell rang, it didn't look like he was going to get much out of saving them either. He was probably going to end up dead.

If I wanted to do something that mattered, then I was definitely living in the wrong place and the wrong time. Nobody cared here. Nobody cared now. The last people to really care about anything important were the draft dodgers, who moved here from America so they didn't get sent to die, in Vietnam I think, and that was more than forty years ago. They didn't exactly do anything heroic either. They just came here to hide out and raise hippie babies out in the woods.

Still, watching that movie made me kind of wish that there was *something* I cared about; that I could make a difference with – even if it was fighting for a place for bears to live.

As I left the class, I thought about how if I died tomorrow, it wouldn't make one difference to the world. You know the thought that comes next, don't you? The cliché *I wish it were me with cancer, and not Emma*. I didn't exactly wish that. Let's be honest, who really means it when they say that? But I kind of thought the universe would be just that little bit fairer if it were the case.

The universe wasn't fair though. It was just a giant hat with names thrown into it – for the bad stuff and the good. That boy Farley was deluded if he thought otherwise.

I made it through three classes before bailing. I actually might have made it a whole day, because I really didn't want to see Emma or my mother; Mom for the obvious reason that she couldn't even remember my birthday and Emma for more couldn't-put-my-finger-on-it reasons. Sure, I'd been horrible to her the other day, but generally Emma didn't hold a grudge. It was more a feeling that that I had, and didn't like. Her chemo being stopped. Mom coming home for the night and then going back to the hospital so early. It all made me a bit jumpy. Something was up and I didn't want to know about it.

In the end I wanted to see Tracey less though. I hated disappointing her, but I also just couldn't face hanging out with her either. I put it down to the jumpiness thing. It made sense, right? So I sent her a text as soon as I was out of third class, saying that I had to go to the hospital. I didn't expand on it. I didn't need to; she sent me back a long-winded text saying that she understood and hoped I was okay and that she was there for me whenever I needed her. She always did that to me. It was bad enough that I lied to her and avoided her – and I didn't even know why – without her totally forgiving me and *still* being there for me without fail.

The weather wasn't so bad, so I thought I'd walk down to the park to have a nose around, see if anything had been left behind by the protesters. It was something to do and now that I was thinking about it, I wasn't exactly sure what the tent city had all been about. Maybe there would be some left over flyers or something.

I was four blocks away from the park when the universe threw me a massive curveball. Four blocks from the park was the bus stop, where the bus departed from Kendal to Red River. And the bus was parked there.

That obviously isn't the curveball. I knew the bus stopped there. I caught the bus to Red River there probably three or four days a week. The curveball was that Farley, yes THAT Farley, was walking toward the bus. It isn't like I could have mistaken him for anyone else. Impossible.

What should have happened was that I kept walking. This wasn't the bus I ever took. I always waited for at least the next one. I wasn't even sure whether it was the direct bus, or the 'milk run' as it was called – don't ask me why, maybe milk used to be delivered by bus, I just know that the milk run goes everywhere, zig zagging through every little side village. It takes forever to get to Red River on it.

And I had a plan for the day. A plan that did not involve getting on the 12.20 bus. In any case, no matter how many classes I went to or didn't go to in a day, I NEVER took the 12.20 bus to Red River. NEVER. That was a personal rule.

Guess what I did? It was that kind of day. Like a lamb to the slaughter (like I know what that means) I followed Mr Disco Hair right on to the bus. As if I regularly boarded the 12.20pm bus from Kendal to Red River.

There was something about him that made me want to

see him more — literally just look at him. He definitely stood out, but in this really quiet, fluid way. He walked like he had all of the time in the world, some sort of black case slung over his shoulder. You know how some people seem to ooze 'look at me!'? This guy didn't seem like that at all. More like he couldn't help standing out.

As soon as I was up the stairs, taking out my student transport card to show the driver, I wanted to turn around and get off. When I faced the rows of passengers, everyone was looking at me. Okay, there were only five people on the bus, but they were all looking at me. They weren't just looking at me, they were frowning at me. There was probably some sort of rule about taking the 12.20 — like it was a members only run, the same people every day, where they held a secret meeting, because nobody would suspect a meeting on a bus. I was going to ruin it.

Except that Farley was on the bus too, and he couldn't be part of the secret club. He was passenger number six, and yesterday he had not been on the 12.20 bus, because he had been talking to me at the café after that time. Plus, he *wasn't* staring at me, which was oddly calming considering I had essentially just followed him on to the bus, expecting that he would immediately do just that.

Maybe it was because he wasn't looking at me that I just took a big breath and walked past him, past all of the secret club members, to the third row from the back, and sat down, slouching as low as I could. What was the big deal about getting on an earlier bus anyway? Red River was at least a bigger town – I could follow my ten-minute-each-store browsing rule and be sure to waste enough time before I could go to the hospital.

I was only getting on the bus because it happened to be there just as I was passing. Definitely.

Only – telling myself all of this didn't make me forget that Mr Disco-hair was in a seat not so far ahead of me. I was probably just blowing it all out of proportion though – that whole *the universe has sent you to me* stuff. It wasn't as if he had even noticed when I got on the bus. He likely didn't even remember me. He probably had random talks like that with everyone he ran into.

I pulled out one of my binders and didn't even pretend to myself that I was going to catch up on any of my assignments. I needed to draw instead. First, the old man just ahead of me across the aisle. He had these little wisps of hair on the top of his head that reminded me of baby bird feathers. They kind of fluttered when he moved his head, which he did a lot because he kept almost falling asleep and then he'd catch himself and snap his head up. But then he must have felt me watching him and he looked back to give me a glare that didn't match his cute, baby-bird hair at all. I tried to glare back, but I'm not very good at being angry at people I don't even know, so I waved hello instead and turned my page over in case he looked.

So then I just doodled, the frost patterns from the bus window the other day duplicating themselves on my page. Thoughts stopped as the intricate swirls and shards of frost covered the page. Jack Frost emerged in the corner, casting the patterns from his fingers, a mass of curly hair to match the frost fronds. Unruly, like my mind.

'Is that supposed to be me?'

My hand shot across the page, leaving Jack Frost with one massive, single strand of hair, the only one a straightener had touched. I looked up to find Farley's face peering over the seat at me. If my heart had begun to calm down, and that was doubtful, it was definitely doing double time again.

'Excuse me?' I struggled to find some sort of words that would put him in his place and make me feel in control again.

'I highly doubt it is of anyone else around here.' Farley pointed over the seat at my Jack Frost that I had to admit, though I didn't mean it to, had hair not dissimilar to Farley's. 'Mind if I sit beside you?'

He didn't wait for me to answer, sliding into the seat beside me, before I could protest. Would I have protested? It isn't exactly like I was being very successful pretending to myself that I was trying to avoid him. Though there didn't seem to be any good reason why I shouldn't be avoiding him.

'Let me see that?' He took the binder from my hands, and brought it right up to his face. 'Before you comment, because I'm reasonably sure I feel a comment forming in your pretty head, yes, I am practically blind without my contact lenses, a new pair of which I am awaiting in the mail, and no, I'm far too vain to even consider wearing my glasses.'

'The comment I was forming, for your information, was that it's slightly presumptuous to think I want to spend an hour in your company.' I knew that sounded ridiculous before I opened my mouth. I wanted to take my binder back, with its doodle. I felt weirdly exposed with it in his hands.

'A moment.' He raised a finger, and brought the book even closer to his face.

'It isn't you. Don't you recognise Jack Frost when you see him?' I tried to salvage some bit of pride and privacy.

'Funny thing about that, I've never met the mythical man.' But he didn't laugh at me; his expression remained dead serious as he studied my squiggles.

So I shut up, for once in my life. It was a weird kind of scared I felt while I studied Farley study my doodling. Kind of like there was an electric wire just in reach, and all I had to do was grab it to have a massive jolt of electricity run through my body. I didn't know what would happen next. I *always* knew what would happen next – even when I hated what would happen next. Even when what happened next was basically nothing, which was most of the time.

I just shut up and studied Farley instead. He was odd look-ing – no doubt about that. Obviously there was that hair. It took up the width of his seat, and sprung onto the back of mine as well. But maybe his hair just seemed so big because it was too wild for his slight, flawless face. And his eyes were so big in his fine face. Every surface was smooth, except for tiny lines from the corner of his eyes. Laugh lines. Did that make him older? He seemed older. But he couldn't be *that* old. Not more than twenty, that was certain.

Or maybe he just seemed not familiar, like I couldn't quite place him in any of the boxes I was used to putting people in. It wasn't just his colour either; there were plenty of shades represented around here, even if few were as deep brown as Farley's shade. It was more that not all of him went in any one box. I wanted to take my notebook back, to draw him, to see if I could figure him out that way.

'Not bad, not bad at all,' he said, as he finally handed my book back to me. 'What else have you got?'

'What do you mean? You want to see my English notes next? Don't you have your own homework to do?' I wasn't sure that he did, but there had been all of those books on the table at the café. Though they weren't books on our school curriculum. I don't know why it bothered me so much that

I couldn't figure him out, not even his age. Why did I care if he was sixteen or twenty?

He didn't say anything for a moment, just looked at me in that way he had the day before. Not in a look me up and down sort of way, more like he was trying to see through me, or through something anyway.

'This is going to take a while isn't it?' he said finally.

'What is?'

'It's going to take a while to chip away this ice exterior of yours.'

'Do you not know how to properly introduce yourself?' I was getting a bit tired of this cryptic talk. 'I am supposed to somehow be fated to meet you, but so far all you have done is make a bunch of bullshit statements, without telling me one thing about yourself.'

'Okay, fair enough. I am going to give you the abridged version of my life. After that, if you don't think I am too much of a psycho, maybe you can show me a little more of your art. Does that seem reasonable?'

I just nodded, because if I was going to be on the bus with him for another fifty minutes I at least wanted to know something about him. I didn't mention that I didn't have any art in the first place, just scribbles in the margins of my copy books.

'So you know my name obviously. My full handle is Farley Johnston. We'll work backwards, yeah? So, I've been back in the area for twenty-three days now. I guess you could say I came back on a bit of a quest.' He stopped there. 'This is the part where you ask me 'what kind of a quest?'' he said, 'If we are going to go through the motions of proper social etiquette, then you have to play along too.'

'Fine. What kind of a quest, Farley Johnston?'

'A quest to find out who my mother was. I guess to find out who I might be.'

'Not to burst your bubble, but in my estimation, knowing your mother doesn't exactly tell you much about yourself.' I was curious though; this wasn't your average what-is-happening-Saturday-night conversation. 'But how come you don't know her?'

'Dead. Dead for seventeen years – since I was one.'

'Oh. Sorry, I guess?' Well that answered my question of how old he was anyway.

'It's kind of old news by now, but thanks for the sentiment. Well done on the appropriate social skills, by the way. Asking questions, appearing interested. How am I doing myself?'

'Hmmm. A little heavy on the personal details, a little light on complaining about the latest tax increases. I'll forgive you that though. Small talk bores me.'

'See, I could tell you and I were soul mates. Meaningless verbal exchanges should be banned.'

'Hold on to your pants, Farley. A few minutes of talking is hardly enough to judge whether we are soul mates. You might find I have no soul. Tell me more, so I can find out if *you* have one.'

It actually felt okay talking to Farley. I didn't have to think about what I said. He basically didn't seem capable of being offended.

'Oh, I must have a soul,' he bantered. 'I think it is a pre-requisite for children born to hippy mothers. All of that free love stuff.'

'So I was right! Were you part of that protest?' It was only when that was out of my mouth that I realised that maybe I had been thinking of Farley, at least a little, since we'd met. Farley didn't miss that either, a grin filling his face.

'Even more hippie than that. I think my parents were the last of the actual, true Smithstown commune.'

I knew the place. Well, I didn't *know* it. I'd never been there, but it had been kind of controversial a few years before, when there had been a big court case. The land had been government land, and they had never had permission to stay there, or to build houses and stuff on it. Still, nobody had said anything about it for like thirty years. It's not like anyone is stuck for space around here.

But then, the commune started to cut down some of the trees and sell them. Just a few, here and there, using tradi-tional tools and horses to pull them out.

The problem was, each tree was worth thousands – really old growth trees, huge. They were making a killing. Just about the time there didn't seem to be a whole lot of those old growth trees to cut down anywhere else. One of the big logging companies noticed and wanted a contract with the government to cut them down. That's when the government tried to evict them. It was too late; squatter's rights stood up in court.

'But isn't it still there?' I was definitely forgetting to be dismissive. 'You were born there?'

'Technically, yes, on both accounts. It's one of the few communes that have survived, but there is nothing communal about it—unless you count land ownership, and yes I was born there, though I don't think you will find any records to say that.'

'Kind of weird, but at least less boring than my life. Two parents, two kids, in one regular, small town.'

'It's a funny thing, where you are born, isn't it?' he said. 'You don't really have a choice about it, yet it has a way of determining the rest of your life if you let it.'

I knew *exactly* what he was saying.

'But in my case, where I was born seems to have caused extra difficulty – or at least it did when my mom died. She was Canadian. Dad was, well still is I guess, American, but getting me back to America, with no birth certificate, and no mother to vouch for my birth ... tricky. I think dealing with all of the bureaucracy beat any hippie notions straight out of him. He ended up going back to school to study law.'

'Me too! I mean – my mom went back to school to study law.' For once I didn't feel the need to downplay the fact.

'Jane, we are in danger of having a socially appropriate conversation now,' Farley warned. 'Are you sure you are prepared for all of this sharing?'

I guess I was prepared for that because we just kept talking for a while. About stuff. Small talk I suppose, but it didn't feel like small talk. It felt like I was filling up with real words, real contact with someone for the first time in months.

Farley told me about coming to stay for a year with his mom's best friend. About how he had fought with his dad about it, but how his dad had relented in the end, as long as Farley agreed to sign up for correspondence college courses and promise that he wouldn't 'drop out of society' like his dad had for years.

I told Farley about my family, about Verwood, and how nothing ever happened in it. I thought about not mentioning Dell – I don't know why – but in the end I did tell him.

'Just so we are clear on what kind of soul mates we may or may not be, I've already got a boyfriend,' I said, and it didn't feel presumptuous to say it.

'Already knew that,' he said.

'How?' There was certainly no promise ring on my finger. Dell would not have dared to even think of one of those.

'You were mostly okay with me looking over your portrait of myself. If you were lusting after me, you would have burned that paper before showing it to me.'

'First of all – how many times do I have to tell you that I was drawing Jack Frost and not you,' I said. 'Second, who says I would be lusting after you if I *didn't* have a boyfriend. I'd say you aren't my type at all.' The truth was, he wasn't any type I had ever met.

'Oh, I'm your type all right. But that's okay. Life is long.'

We were nearing Red River by this time, and I wondered where Farley was going. Maybe I would have asked him, but as I went to put my history binder back in my backpack, Farley remembered that I hadn't shown him any art.

'Hand the books over. We had a deal.'

'We only had a deal if I think you're not a psycho. I'm not convinced you aren't,' I said. 'Besides, I'm sorry to disappoint, but I don't have real art. Just doodles.'

'Have you not seen any of Picasso's early stuff? All doodles,' he said, and dug into my bag to retrieve another two binders.

I hadn't realised how much doodling I had been doing lately. Every margin was filled. There was way more doodling than notes. Farley flipped through the pages, bringing the binders up to his face with each turned page, which kind of made him look like an old man. Only without the old man smell, more musky-clean, with no cologne to mask it. Dell always wore cologne.

Thinking that made me feel self-conscious, like he might

be reading my thoughts, until I saw that he was actually, no bullshit, still intensely looking at my squiggles and lines, where there should have been school work. He looked through every binder I had, twice, before he would let me put them away. I kept trying to take them from him, and he kept turning away from me until he had finished with each one.

Finally, all binders were safely away and I felt dressed again. We were nearly at the station.

'So, you're good at faces. You're getting the essence of people. You need to work on more detail though, a little more perspective. Where's your camera? You should be taking tons of pictures of people. Then, sit down and draw them until you can see every line in your sleep.'

'What, are you some kind of master painter, who knows about art?' I meant it as a joke.

'Not exactly. But I guess the arts are kind of my thing. I'm told I am kind of good at the violin.' He held up the case that was at his feet. So that was what was in there.

'Is that why you are coming to Red River, to take lessons?'

The bus had come to a stop now, and we joined the others in the aisle, waiting for the door to open.

'Not exactly,' he said. 'I'm kind of teaching some classes.'

'Right.' Here he was, stepping out of any box I tried to build for him. 'And you know a lot about art and music too?'

'I kind of have no choice. I absorb it like a sponge.'

I wanted to ask him more about that, but he was gone as soon as we were off the bus. He just waved and smiled – and left. So much for social etiquette.

It felt okay though. I'd had one of the most honest exchanges with anyone in ages, and I hadn't scared him off. I'd see him again.

It was only as I was walking toward the hospital that I started to question the honest part. There was a little thought niggling at the back of my mind that kept trying to come to the front. I hadn't once mentioned Emma and her illness – the reason I was heading to Red River. It hadn't seemed important at the time. It hadn't come up. We had been talking about ourselves, what mattered to us. I was sure that Farley had whole reams of things that he had not shared with me.

So, it was normal right, to not mention it?

Still, it made me feel a little guilty. Like here I was, with a promise of a life, while Emma was stuck inside the hulking institution that kept growing as I moved toward it. And I hadn't even thought she was important enough to mention.

It wasn't like she would know, or even care. It's just that sometimes I missed the sister that she might have been growing into – if she had a chance to, outside of being the perpetual patient, I mean. Maybe if she had gone to the high school this year we would have started to have friends in common. Maybe I would have had a reason to try harder – so that she would have someone to look up to.

Instead, there had been this nothingness; this void. It wasn't Emma's fault, but the cancer had become a pretty big black hole in my life.

For the first time since I could remember though, I felt like something could be different. It felt good, and I didn't want to share Emma's illness with this newness. I wanted this feeling all to myself. This was my life and my feeling. That was allowed wasn't it?

Something was wrong. I could feel it even though both Mom and Emma smiled big, toothy grins when I walked in. Mom's chair – the one with her pillow and blanket from home, with her paperback books piled on the floor beside it – was nearly two feet back from Emma's bed. Usually Mom couldn't get close enough to Emma.

'What's up?' I didn't expect an honest answer, and I didn't get one.

'Your birthday is what's up!' said Mom, which elicited a glare from Emma. *An actual glare.* I didn't think Emma was capable of it. It didn't really count though, focused as it was on Mom's back as she left the room to retrieve a cake with sixteen unlit candles on it. The cake was one of those ones from the supermarket, no writing or anything.

'Sorry, we can't light them here,' Mom apologised.

Emma still hadn't said anything. When Mom went back out to find a knife to cut the cake, she took a paper bag from under her blankets and handed it to me.

'This is from me,' she said and then added for emphasis, '*Just* me.'

Inside was a bracelet with intricately painted beads. From a distance, it looked like a very pretty bracelet, but when I looked closely, there was a tiny figure on each bead. *Star Wars* figures. I didn't care that her present was two years out of date. I hadn't been obsessed with *Star Wars* for ages.

'I'll play monopoly with you any time, Ems,' I said, pulling her little body in for a hug.

'I had lots more ideas, but I couldn't do much from here. The lady who does jewellery making on Tuesdays with the kids hooked me up with the beads.'

I wondered when she had stopped seeing herself as one of 'the kids'.

'Here we go!' Mom said, coming back in with a knife. 'Now, Dad will have your proper present for you when you get home, but we had to have a bit of celebration here too.' She handed us each a slice of cake on blue, hospital paper towel. Emma had gone silent and sullen again, but Mom was ignoring it, or not noticing, filling the silence herself.

'Mmmm. That's very good cake,' she said. 'Much better

than any I make. What do you think, Jane? I got the black forest because I know you love cherries.'

'Thanks, Mom. Delicious,' I managed, though I could tell she wasn't really waiting for my response anyway. Emma left her cake untouched, and Mom didn't say a word about it. I ate mine, though Mom was wrong – even her worst cakes were better than this.

'I got us a DVD to watch together as well, and popcorn. We'll have a proper girls' afternoon.'

I felt like I was at the Mad Hatter's tea party the way Emma and Mom were acting. All upside down. Emma always tried to please, even when you knew she didn't want to, and Mom was like me, not able to hide how she felt, no matter how hard she tried. She was trying to do it now, but she wasn't that good at it. She forgot to keep the happy face once the movie was on.

It was an old movie, one of those that you flip past on TV because you have seen it so many times before. I could tell that Emma was tired, because she laid back and watched it anyway, ending her angry stand-off with Mom. Whatever was going on between them had taken its toll on her.

I looked over to find Mom staring at the wall, so lost in her thoughts that she had forgotten that she was with us. The happy façade was gone. She looked – old. Everything about her sagging and tired. More than that though, I had never seen her look as sad as she looked right then. I watched her for a long time, and that sadness did not lift one bit.

We might have stayed like that until the end of the movie. I had even curled onto the end of Emma's bed to watch it when I got tired of watching Mom. And then, I was being splattered with water – well I thought it was water until I sat up to see blood pouring out of Emma's nose.

'I'm alright,' she gurgled, even as she seemed to be bleeding to death. Mom didn't seem any more assured than I felt though, rushing to grab paper towels, and pressing the button for the nurse. There was blood everywhere.

'Oh, Hon,' the nurse who came in said, taking over from Mom.

'It's okay,' Emma still managed, though it was looking less and less okay to me.

'Head forward, pinch your nose. We're okay.' Every move the nurse made was steady and sure. The blood was stopping, or at least I couldn't see it through the gauze the nurse had held over Emma's nose.

'She can't take this, can she?' Mom was talking to the nurse as if Emma and I weren't even there.

'It's just one nose bleed. We'll see what the doctor says tomorrow,' the nurse said. 'He'll do his best to spare…'

Mom cleared her throat so loudly that there was no disguising the fact that it was a signal for the nurse to stop talking.

'Spare what?' I asked. Nobody answered me.

'What?' I tried again.

'Emma is just on a new medication, that's all, Jane,' Mom said, but she didn't look at me. 'The doctor just wants to make sure she is okay.'

She was lying. I wished that Emma's face wasn't hidden in gauze, so I could have seen her expression. Did she know what was up?

I knew that this was not 'nothing to worry about' when Dr Jonathan came in the room. Doctors didn't just come around at any old time, not even blue coats. Rounds are in the mornings. Plus, he didn't just stroll in like he was stopping by for a chat; he rushed in like he had been called.

'So, this is an odd one,' he said, as he did what every doctor did first – pull his stethoscope out of his pocket. With doctors it was always the stethoscope, with nurses it was the blood pressure cuff. I suspected neither mattered much most of the time. They just needed something to do when they didn't have a clue where to start.

'Jane, can you go get a couple of drinks from the machine?' Mom asked, reaching for her purse to get some money.

'Right now? You can't be serious?'

'Please. Just give the doctor a minute.'

'What is going on? What are you not saying? Is she dying?'
I blurted. I knew I shouldn't be so blunt, especially with
Emma still under a pile of gauze, but I couldn't help it. Mom
was being so vague, and it wasn't fair. Sure enough, she was
not-so-subtly trying to give Dr Jonathan a signal to shut up.
I don't know how she thought I would miss her waving her
hand in front of her mouth like that.

He got the message. I could tell by the way he looked
straight back at her and kept her gaze for a second or two
before answering.

'You don't need to worry, Jane.' He remembered my name,
I'd give him points for that; most doctors didn't.

'Do I not need to worry? Oh, good. Glad you have this
whole thing under control, and I'm delighted that I don't
need to know anything about it. Sure, I'm only the sister.
And obviously, my mother feels it's much more important
that I go fetch drinks for her precious other daughter than
hang out here finding out if there actually is something to
worry about.'

'Jane! Stop this right now!' Mom hissed.

'I hate this place! I come here every fucking day, and I
hate it. The least you could do is stop treating me like I am
some kind of unpaid childminder, fetcher of stuff . . .' I knew
everyone was looking at me, but I couldn't stop. 'I don't even
have a chair in this room!'

Okay, it wasn't the most articulate of rants. But the chair

part was true. There was only one. For Mom.

I walked out before my heart could stop racing, knowing that any second now I was going to want to take back every one of those words. It was embarrassing how I couldn't shut myself up sometimes. I seemed to be getting worse at spouting off the first words that came into my head.

It had looked like Emma was going to bleed to death though and even out of the room I couldn't stop picturing all of that blood.

It was just a nose bleed I told myself. No worse than the vomiting. Just another in a list of side effects Emma had to endure. So why did it make me feel so scared? Why did something feel so wrong?

I calmed down after I wandered around the ground floor of the hospital for a bit, before finding a machine and heading back upstairs with the drinks I'd been sort-of sent for. I didn't want to be here anymore though. I thought I would drop Emma and Mom their cans of soda and go.

I was just about to Emma's room, when Dr Jonathan came out of the door. He could have headed down the hallway in the other direction, but instead he stopped, and looked straight at me, and he was going to tell me the truth. I could see it in his eyes.

'You are right. Things are not exactly as we would like them right now, but there isn't anything to panic about.' He waited, probably to make sure I wasn't going to start ranting again. 'Emma might be having a nose bleed because kids just get them sometimes. But that isn't likely, is it?'

I shook my head.

'This isn't the cancer though. It could be a reaction to the drug we are giving her. This one is giving Emma grief.'

'Okay.' I could feel my heart slowing finally. At least one person would tell me the truth when I wanted to hear it.

It wasn't until I was on the bus going home that I thought about Dell. He had sent me three messages by that time. HAPPY BIRTHDAY TO JANE xoxoxo. U COMING OVER? And finally, WHERE ARE U NOW? CAN U COME OVER? Dell didn't message me much. It just wasn't what we did.

Funny, I hadn't actually thought of him as part of my birth-day at all, if you could call it a birthday. All I really wanted to do was crawl into my bed and stay there. Even before losing the plot with Mom it had been a fairly crap day. I just wanted it to be over.

The only good part had been talking with Farley. It felt like seeing Dell would ruin that somehow.

I messaged Dell back: TIRED. HOW ABOUT TOMOR-ROW?

PLEASE? He messaged back straight away.

Fine. I'd go over.

Maybe this is a good time to explain my relationship with Dell. We've been together fifteen months now. See, I am not completely indifferent; I know our anniversaries. And I am aware that everyone around me thinks I am the luckiest girl on earth. It's probably the biggest reason why there's such a rift between Brenda and Aishling and myself. They are jealous. I know they are. If there was a choice, Brenda would totally be with Dell and not Stan. She doesn't *think* that, but she feels it. Tracey and I may have spent most of grade eight secretly wanting to be with Dell, but Brenda had made no secret of her intentions, practically stalking him the whole year. She had never quite forgiven me for being the one to land him in the end, though why it was me has always been a bit of a mystery to us all.

Poor Dell. I'm saving him from them. He doesn't know it, but if Brenda got her claws in his sweet hide, he'd wake up at forty-five and wonder what the hell had happened to him. She has her whole life mapped out – from the big wedding, to the two kids, to the bungalow and landscaped garden. To her, he would be a commodity, an acquisition, kind of like a

glorified garden gnome. Granted, he'd be a very good looking acquisition, but I'm afraid that it might only take ten
years for him to lose that value. And I'd like to see him loved
for a bit more time than that.

Not that I picked Dell as my boyfriend. I didn't pick
anyone.

There was this softball tournament the summer before
last that Tracey dragged me to. Well that isn't true; I think I
actually wanted to go to it. Emma had been at home then,
in remission, and looking back I'm sure that it had felt like
I could begin to live again. It's hard to imagine now, but
I'm sure that I thought the cancer was over. Lately, I have a
hard time remembering how I felt when times were good. It
doesn't feel like they ever were good, but if I think about it,
I think they must have been.

If I really think about it, I can see Tracey and I that weekend, perched on the top bench behind first base, watching the
games. The sun is shining and the shorts and t-shirts we are
wearing look 'first-thing-thrown-on' even though it took us
ages to decide what to wear. Well, ages for Tracey to decide
for both of us, because she has always been my fashion guru,
since I have no idea about clothes myself. I can see this air
of possibility hanging over us, making us almost magnets for
people to look at. I can see that, but I can't remember how
it felt anymore.

Anyway, I ended up at this dance on the Saturday night,

this barn dance. It literally was in a barn. There was a band playing and there was a makeshift bar behind these bales of hay. I was just hanging out with Tracey, waiting for the music to start, and to see whether there was anything to stay for. When you live in a small town, unless it's specifically designated a 'house wrecker', any party is for every age – which means that you are never too sure whether it's going to turn into an entirely geriatric event, or offer a bit of interest for those of us under twenty.

The band had started to play, the usual country and western cover tunes that bands always started with at these things. Tracey was sitting beside me, not really just hanging out at all, but on the vigilant look out for any of the guys from the out-of-town teams. She had a couple of them in particular earmarked as potentials. Not the best looking ones – Tracey never aimed that high – but the sweet-looking ones. She didn't say it, but I think that she hoped that they wouldn't frighten her as much and she would be at least be able to open her mouth.

But it wasn't any of them that came up to us. It was Dell, and one of his friends. We pretty much assumed they were just hanging out with us because there was no one else better around yet. I mean, they'd known us all their lives; it didn't mean anything that they were hanging out with us. It might have just been an ordinary night. There was no way I would have believed that Dell actually *liked* me. That was so far out of my idea of possible that he didn't even make me nervous.

So there hadn't been any pressure to try to be cool or anything, which was why we probably ended up together in the first place. When Dell came over with bottles of cola for all of us, I held mine up and said the dorkiest thing. *May the force be with you*, because, yes, I tend to get a bit obsessed with certain movies, even if it's sometimes years out of step with everyone else.

I twisted the beads of the bracelet Emma had made for me, thinking of that night. It turns out Dell knew a lot about *Star Wars*. It turns out he was happy to talk about that topic all night, which turned into kissing, which was probably his aim all along, because I don't remember talking about *Star Wars* much once we'd been together for a couple of weeks.

That's what happens though, isn't it? You think you have this great connection with someone, just because they say something you care about, but really, it's just an excuse to go off and make out with them. It's like those mating calls that birds make. Once you are with someone, there isn't any need to keep making the same noises.

Still. I had really liked Dell. I know that I should *still* really like him. There's nothing not to like. Okay, so there are some limitations to him. He is a little socially awkward, in a way that you only notice after you have known him for a while. And he doesn't dance – not at all, not even in that drunk, end of night kind of way. And conversations with him are sort of limited to the immediate happenings. But none of that is really bad. It actually makes it pretty comfortable to be around him.

But sometimes, like now, when I didn't even care enough to go home to change into something nicer, or at least less blood stained, before going to his house, it crossed my mind that maybe Dell was just convenient to be with. Being with him meant that I never had to think about what I was doing on the weekend. I never had to think at all—I just had to roll through his window and into a world where the screen ruled. It told me what to think. Easy.

I liked that Dell mostly liked to stay in, and didn't try to drag me to parties. Once, only once, he told me that his dad had drank enough alcohol for the both of their lifetimes. I could see his point. Alan wasn't known for being a 'happy' drunk. People kind of avoided him as soon as he had more than one beer in him.

I liked that I could be going over to Dell's house without a stitch of makeup and just thrown-on school clothes, and Dell wouldn't notice. I knew what to expect, and that was maybe a life saver for me. At Dell's, I didn't have to make up rules for myself to make it through each hour, or pretend that I actually gave a shit about conversations so that I didn't offend anyone.

So, yeah, maybe I wished a little that I felt something more, if only so that Brenda's jealously wouldn't be so, so wasted.

But on the scale of most shitty to pretty good, Dell was on the pretty good end of my life.

That was about what I was thinking when I went to open the window to the basement rec room and found it locked. Dell never locked the window. We don't exactly have a huge theft problem in Verwood.

I was rapping on the window for the third time, when Dell opened the front door wearing a suit. Well, it was as close to a suit as Dell owns – a button down shirt, a jacket and his best pair of jeans. I had only seen him in that sort of get up once before, at his uncle's wedding. I'd thought he looked pretty hot in it then.

For some reason, seeing him in it now just made me think of Farley. I imagined Farley standing beside him in his brown corduroys and huge Guatemalan hippie-hoodie. It was hard to tell what kind of body was under that, but his hands were beautiful. It was only now, with Dell standing in front of me instead, that I remembered how beautiful they were.

'I hope you're not dressed for a funeral!' I said, looking to see if his dad's truck was in the drive before I went in the front door. It wasn't. Usually Dell would have at least attempted to reply with equal sarcasm, but he just stood there, shuffling from foot to foot, until I reached the steps.

'It's your birthday,' he said, as if I didn't know. 'I wanted to, you know, make it special.'

Special. I didn't like the sound of this coming from Dell. I peeked in the door suspiciously. What if he had a bunch of people in there, and here I was still wearing clothes splattered with my sister's blood?

It was worse though. At first I wasn't sure what it was because the hallway was pretty dark, but when I looked closely, what I saw were rose petals. Red rose petals leading down the hall and to the kitchen. It was all I could do to stop myself from getting a broom and sweeping them up. It was so wrong in so many ways. Blood-red petals. Roses. Red roses. Leading where? This couldn't lead anywhere good.

The rational part of me could see Dell buying the roses, tearing them apart and putting down these petals, not because *he* thought it would make my birthday special, but because someone had told him it would. It wasn't his fault that it only made me think of a trail of blood.

So I smiled. I bit my tongue. I mean, I really bit my tongue, until I tasted iron flooding my mouth. It was a sensation I could hold on to. If I didn't hold onto something I wouldn't be able to follow that blood trail through the kitchen and down the stairs.

Dell was right behind me, grinning like a Cheshire cat. No, that's not right. I think I was grinning like the Cheshire cat. Dell was smiling more like a big yellow Labrador. I tried to imagine him like one, so that I would only want to hug him, instead of flailing out and hitting him as I ran the other way.

Down the stairs, with the yellow Labrador right behind me.

There wasn't anybody down there though. And there wasn't some mad quartet ready to serenade us, while we ate lobster and sipped champagne, either.

There was just a little box, obviously wrapped by some shop owner, and a bouquet of roses. Dell handed me both of these as soon as I had collapsed on the sofa in relief.

'Come on, Jane, open it,' he urged, reminding me even more of an eager puppy. He really was so sweet.

I swallowed blood and tried to look as sweetly back at him, though I was starting to feel like throwing up now.

I was careful with taking the wrapping paper off. Silver paper with black tiger stripes through it. Deep purple bow. God, what if it was a ring? The thought made blood drain to my feet. I felt it dripping down my veins, leaving ice in its wake.

Inside, nestled in sliver satin though was ... at first I wasn't sure. It was a pendent. A big circular pendant. On a chain. It was chiselled gold, with a fairy on a toadstool inside the circle, so shiny that even the meagre light from the bulb on the ceiling made every carved detail glint.

Dell wanted me to put on now. He was actually holding his hands out to help me put it on. And I let him; the heavy pendant knocked against my chest like a medal as he tried to fasten the clasp at my neck.

It was a horrid thing – unless of course you were mad into fairies, and I don't think that I had ever mentioned anything like this to Dell. But it was a medal all right. It was a medal to reward me for using Dell so spectacularly for so long.

'Do you like it?' His face was lit up in anticipation. I'm sure it had cost him a fortune. And he still hadn't noticed that I hadn't said a word. I still couldn't say a word. I nodded and smiled my Cheshire cat grin instead. Which made him smile back at me in the most genuine way.

'I wasn't sure if you wanted to do anything,' he said, still sitting up straight, in his good clothes. I wasn't used to seeing him out of his slumped position on the sofa. There was only one thing 'to do' in Verwood if you were underage and couldn't go to the pub, and that was to go for dinner at Shirley's. I really couldn't face that though.

Poor Dell. He had gone to so much effort. Everyone had. Even Mom had tried her best in the end. It didn't help. All I felt was tired.

I smiled at him again, but I could feel a sting in the corners of my eyes.

'I'd really like to stay in,' I risked saying, 'with you.'

I nearly felt all defences let the tears through when Dell

107

grinned back at me and nodded. I was so relieved.

Dell ordered pizza instead. It's our only delivery choice in Verwood, but that is okay because it's pretty good pizza. And I kept feeling relief until it came. Everything was back to normal. Dell flipped through the television channels, and then turned on the game console when there was nothing on.

But I couldn't seem to quite find our groove again. Usually I filled the empty spaces with banter. My voice was some-how gone. The circle hanging from my neck seemed very heavy. Very, very heavy and I couldn't stop thinking of that sensation. I picked up another piece of pizza, even though I had only eaten the pepperoni off the first piece. I wasn't hungry, but I needed to have something in my hands to stop myself from ripping the chain from my neck.

Dell had his eyes firmly on the screen now, immersed in running from the sniper who was firing at him from the burned out building across the street. All I had to do was sit there, like every other night. Sit there and enjoy this really good pizza. The medal was ruining everything.

I watched Dell play, watched his hands automatically find the buttons that were the extension of his on-screen world.

His fingers were too short. Not for the game, they worked just fine for that. But just, too short. I felt annoyed at myself for even thinking this. What the fuck had I ever cared about fingers for? I didn't. But I couldn't help being irritated by them.

'Dell, can we watch something instead?' I couldn't just sit there and think about how Dell had the wrong hands. I had to stop thinking all together.

Dell switched off the console and turned the television back on. There was still nothing on, and he kept going through the channels. There were only bad game shows and talk shows on. Every second channel was adverts. Shoes, antacid pills for heartburn, antibacterial spray for cleaning, Zantec for anxiety, Diovan for high blood pressure. Dell was going through the channels again, only faster and all I saw were drugs flashing across the screen now. Companies trying to shove drugs down our throats. Were these the same companies that made the cancer drugs? The ones that made Emma so sick?

Even though Dell had stopped on a channel now, I couldn't stop seeing the ads flash through my mind. It was a strange sensation.

'Stop!' I knew I'd shouted that because Dell jumped so much he practically levitated from the sofa.

'What is up with you, Jane?' he asked when he'd landed again. He squinted at me, as if he were trying to read the fine print. I wish I knew what it said myself. I felt like I had to stop the pictures in my head for anything to make sense.

'Stop! Please stop it!'

'Stop what?'

I knew I wasn't making much sense. I was tired. I just had to calm down. Fast though, because Dell was still squinting at me.

'It's just, it's been a weird day. Can we maybe talk?' I remembered how much better I had felt after talking the whole bus ride with Farley.

Dell turned the television off. Not just with the remote, but by going straight to the button on the television. I suppose it was on the way to his docking station, because he stopped there, scrolling through his files. Dell didn't have a lot of music, but the stuff he did have was mostly metal, which I hated. He knew that, and so we hardly ever listened to music together. He picked the only album that he knew I liked though. Dell was such a decent guy. Thinking this was making the corners of my eyes go all prickly again and I blinked hard as Dell came back to sit on the sofa.

He didn't talk, but just tried to put his arms around me. I'm sure he had pictured a kind of rugged-man-saves-damsel-in-distress moment, but it ended up way more awkward than that. One, you really can't 'sweep' someone into your arms when you come at them from the side. Two, it was me he was trying this move on.

This might be the place to tell you just how sexual, or not sexual, my relationship with Dell was. Everyone totally assumed that we were doing it every other day. We could have been; there wouldn't be anyone noticing to stop us. But we weren't.

It wasn't exactly anyone's business to know that though. Even Tracey wasn't sure what I had or hadn't done with Dell. I was vague about it.

When Dell and I got together, I was completely hot for him. He only had to look at me and I imagined everything I wanted to do with him. The only reason we didn't go all the way in the first few months we were together was that I was fourteen and I guess I was scared. There's this kind of code around Verwood. Any girl who does it before they're fifteen is a complete slut. Don't ask me what the difference between fourteen and fifteen is. Also, I'm not sure why that should have stopped me. It isn't like I had to tell anyone. But anyway, Dell was sixteen, and even though we never talked about it, he knew the code. He could encourage me to ignore that code, but only so much if he was a 'nice' guy. And Dell is most definitely a nice guy – in every sense.

But then what happened, before I reached fifteen – the grey area, not necessarily slutty, but a tad young – was that Emma got really sick again. The cancer showed up in new places; it was the first of her surgeries to remove bits of lung. You know those horror movies where you think the scary parts are all over, and then a hand reaches out of a calm lake to grab the main character? It was like that.

And then there was Grandad. Well, there wasn't Grandad anymore, but, you know, there was thinking about there not being Grandad anymore. Basically, he died. And I didn't like to think about it. I didn't like to think about him at all. He wasn't my favourite person. Or, at least, I wasn't his favourite person. So, yeah, somewhere in there he died.

I say somewhere, because Emma was way more impor- tant at the time, and when I think back about it, that's what I remember. That's what I try to remember. I didn't even go to the funeral because Emma's immune system was too shot to chance her spending an afternoon in the company of everyone else's germs and so I volunteered to stay with her instead. She was a little more important than an old guy who hadn't even liked me much.

Dell thought I didn't want to make out anymore, or do anything else, because I was so upset about it all. Maybe it really was the reason, or what made it happen in the first place anyway. I don't know; all I know is that I kind of stopped feeling anything then. Have you ever tried to kiss a guy who you feel absolutely no attraction to? It would make you gag. It was like one day Dell was this guy I could barely keep from jumping, and almost the very next day he was this guy I only wanted to hug like a teddy bear.

I am probably a complete coward, but I thought that

pushing Dell away every time he tried to put his tongue in my mouth might hasten a breakup. It didn't though. Dell has stuck with me for a whole year – like a brother. Did I already say that he is the nicest guy I have ever met? Except maybe my dad. My dad is pretty much in a tie with Dell for nicest guy.

Tonight, though, I was sixteen. Sixteen is a completely acceptable age to have sex, especially with a boyfriend you have been with for over a year. Hell, there were probably bets on as to whether we'd end up married, because it would be more normal than not around here to marry the guy you are with when you are sixteen. If you think that is a bit twentieth century, you probably haven't grown up in a village of 423 people. Around here, it is the norm.

So, I can't know what exactly was going through Dell's mind, but I knew the rose petals and the beautifully wrapped fairy medal and the music just for me, meant that this night meant something to Dell. Besides acting very strangely, I hadn't exactly steered him from thinking that it meant something to me too. He's not a mind reader.

After the awkward hug, Dell just moved in closer. He managed to get me facing him and then kind of buried his head in my neck. This didn't look like we were gearing up for a talk.

'Jane, you are so special,' he whispered in my ear. His hand was just reaching out, ever so gently, to bring my face around

113

to meet his, and I couldn't bottle up the feeling of needing to get rid of that pendant any longer. Even as I stood up, I hated what I was going to do to Dell. If I would have paused even for a second, I might not have done it, but I didn't. I couldn't. I physically could not stand it anymore. I'd crack up if I did.

I grabbed the pendant and yanked it as hard as I could, snapping the clasp. I put it as gently as I could on the coffee table.

'Dell, I'm not special. This is me, just me.' I took a breath, trying to think of how I could explain, but I didn't under-stand this myself. Everything was starting to buzz and my thoughts were getting drowned in it. 'I can't.'

That was all I could say, and I walked up the steps to the kitchen before I could see my words put an end to his delu-sions.

Before I had gone to Dell's house I'd rang Dad and left a message saying I was doing something with Tracey and the girls. I didn't exactly spell out what that something was, but I did say 'the something' was for my birthday. Since Mom and Dad had clearly forgotten that fact, I thought it would probably cover me. I really didn't want to face any more of the thrown-together family birthday.

I was lying of course. I never told them when I went to Dell's. It isn't that they didn't know that Dell and I were together, but it wasn't a topic I went looking to talk about. I didn't even know if my parents liked him or not. I just know that at one time there would have been lots and lots of discussion if I had said I was going over to some guy's house. Like, what I was planning to do there and which parents were going to be home. Why I should do something else instead. Now all I had to do is not talk about something and it was as if it never happened as far as my parents knew.

I was a bit worried that Dad would still be up when I got in, and I would have to actually lie, rather than just avoid talking, but I shouldn't have worried about that. He hadn't even pretended to stay up by falling asleep in front of the television. All of the lights, except the one in the entrance, had been turned out. I doubted that Dad had wanted to play out my forgotten birthday any more than me.

The little table in the entranceway that was usually hidden by flyers and scarves and whatever else got thrown on the pile, had been cleared off and pulled out from the wall a little. I couldn't pass it without noticing, which was obviously the point because there was a card on it with my name written on the envelope in big letters.

I didn't want it to be my birthday anymore. I didn't want to open this card. By myself.

But I did open it. It would have been kind of difficult to

say that I hadn't seen it.

Fifty dollar notes fluttered to the floor when I pulled the card out. That was my present. Money they didn't even have.

The card said Happy Birthday on the front, and in between the two words Dad had added a little arrow pointing to a '16th' written in pen above. This was a tradition that had been going on since I was one. Emma and I always, always got a card with our birthday age on it. Dad kept them in a shoebox, all in order, marching up the years. Of course, every shop has cards with 'You are 1' on them, which must have been what started Dad's nostalgic habit, but then, he found that some ages were tricky to find. Like, for example, nobody much cares about ninth birthdays. But Dad had always managed to find a card with the right age on it, no matter how tricky the year.

Until now. And the thing is, sixteen is definitely not one of those a tricky ages to find on a card.

My phone was blinking at me before I even got out of bed the next day. I had kind of expected that after leaving Dell's house the way I had the night before. I'd thought maybe if I left it until today I would know what to do about it. I didn't though. Should I apologise? Or was it too late for that?

As I read Dell's eight messages, I couldn't seem to feel what I thought I should. If I was really honest, I didn't feel much. There was this part of me that knew that I had hurt him, and that cared, in the way you care when you hear about an earthquake that kills thousands of people, but they're all far away, and you don't know any of them. Only this was Dell who was hurt. He was five blocks away. And I had been the one to hurt him.

There was one more message that wasn't from Dell. I didn't recognise the number, but I knew exactly who it was from. SEE YOU AT THE CAFÉ TODAY. It wasn't a question. It was one thing to happen to meet and talk but I wasn't sure I liked him looking me up. I was certain I didn't like him telling me what to do.

I didn't respond to any of the messages. In fact, I dropped my phone on my bed before I left. I didn't need it reminding me of things I would rather not think about. I decided right then that I was simply not going to think about things that just made me feel bad. I'd had enough of it.

VIVACE
gioioso

'LIVELY AND FAST, JOYFULLY'

Big, wet snowflakes were falling when I walked out the door. First snowfalls always put me in a good mood. After the last of the autumn leaves turn to mush and there isn't a colour left outside, the first snow fall makes everything pretty again. And quiet. Any chaos stops and everyone gets lost in the newness of it all. It doesn't last of course. Second, third, fourth snowfalls start to bring their own chaos – car accidents, old people falling on the ice, landslides that block the roads. Sleety, ugly, messy snowfalls. It doesn't take every-one long to tire of it all.

But first snowfalls are magic. As I waited for the bus, I looked up, watching the flakes fall in a curtain through the streetlamp that lit the winter, still-dark morning. It was so beautiful.

The weather had changed and something was shifting in my mood as well. For once, I didn't feel tired. If I just kept watching the snow and let any thoughts of Dell or Emma fall away, I almost felt happy. I'd forgotten what that felt like.

'So, did you like it?' Tracey asked. I almost asked '*like what?*'

before I remembered the little box she had slipped into my pocket the day before. Shit. I'd forgotten all about it. I had to think fast.

'It was really late by the time I got home,' I lied. 'I wanted to save it for when I wasn't so tired.' Like opening a present would have been so tiring. It was a terrible lie.

'Oh, I know the file is massive. My mom kept saying that I didn't have to put every picture people gave me on the memory stick, but I thought you could just delete the ones you don't want.'

'Every picture?' She was assuming I had actually opened the present.

'Well, not the ones of when you were really little obviously. I'll add those ones in when your mom has the time to get them to me. I wanted you to have your whole life in your hand.'

'Lunch time. We'll look at them on my laptop together,' I said. And I actually meant it. For the first time in ages I felt like I could make it through a day.

Three classes. Three whole classes. And I have to say, even though I had missed more classes than I had attended lately, I seemed to know more about what was going on in them than a lot of people. I surprised myself as much as my teachers by actually putting up my hand to be part of the classes too. In fact, in math the teacher actually said *'We've heard from you a lot, Jane. Someone else?'* I don't think that I had ever heard that.

I kept my word and met Tracey at lunch. Just the two of us went to Joe's Diner and Tracey insisted on buying me actual lunch – not just a plate of fries.

When I opened up the file on the memory stick (I had to go into the toilet to take the paper off the box, so she wouldn't know I hadn't even opened it yet) I almost cried. In a happy/sad way. Tracey had organised files of pictures from every year of my life. Up until age seven they all just had a note saying 'Coming soon', but every other file had hundreds of pictures. I didn't even know that many pictures had even been taken of me.

Most of them were ones that she and her family had taken. Tracey's mom is one of those people who always seems to have a camera in her hand. So there were a lot of pictures of Tracey and me, but she had also scanned class photos, and gathered pictures from everyone in Verwood it seemed.

It was strange seeing them. It was like looking at someone else's life. Pictures of me camping. Pictures of me playing basketball (that only lasted one season – I was hopeless at it), pictures of me and my pet rabbit (he had lasted a bit longer), pictures of Emma trying to teach me to do a spin at the ice rink (she is as natural on ice as she is on a dance floor).

As Tracey and I scanned through the files, of course I recognised the people, and I remembered most of the things we
were doing, but every picture was still a surprise.

I've heard that we change memories every time we play
them out in our heads. So, like if you remember a favourite
time hundreds of times – the memory might not be what
actually happened in the first place. Maybe you remember it
way better. But what about if you forget altogether? What if
you don't play them out in your head for years? It was like I
was seeing my very own life for the first time. Each memory
the pictures brought up was brand new.

My mind had been on a loop that couldn't see past three
years ago. Like it was one of my dad's old records that he
liked to play, that would get stuck on one song because the
groove was deeper on that one or something. I had forgotten
there were other songs.

'Thank you, Tracey.' I gave her the biggest hug before she
went back to school, and it kind of felt good to get one back.

For once I had asked Tracey if she wanted to skip class with
me. She'd hesitated before saying no. She doesn't like to miss
school; it makes her worry too much about getting caught.

It's one of the reasons I stopped asking her a long time ago. She would go with me, but only if we went to hang out by the river, or stayed on small roads. Even then, she jumped every time she saw a car that she thought she recognised. It had become annoying. At the time I had felt like, what was the point in skipping class if you were not going to enjoy yourself?

But then, that was before I stopped enjoying myself too, more because I was *never* going to 'get caught'. Let's face it, everyone knew, but didn't care. I mean, it had to be fairly obvious that I wasn't there most of the time.

Today though, it was different. I had money in my pocket, and I was going to enjoy every minute of spending it. I knew exactly what I wanted to buy.

There were only two places in Kendal that sold cameras. Neither one seemed very happy to see me. I guess they don't have a lot of teenagers shopping for big ticket items in the middle of a school day. Plus, I had gotten used to trying my best to make sure people in the stores didn't notice me, so I was kind of crap about trying to get them to help me.

There were about ten cameras in my price range and I couldn't tell the difference between any of them. I didn't exactly want to waste Mom and Dad's money either. I may not have been super happy about how they had basically for-gotten my birthday, and maybe if it had been the day before I would have just blown the money to spite them, but today there was ten centimetres of snow covering all those resentments. I was ready for a new start, and I wanted to make the most of the money. It was either that or use it to pay one of the bills marked urgent that kept coming in the door.

So it wasn't because Farley had practically ordered me to meet him that I went to the café. And I was going to make sure that he knew that.

He was sitting at the same table he had been at the first day he had sat me down there. Only this time there were quite a few customers, so his books were under his feet, and there was a couple sharing his table. A tiny message passed through my brain to say it might not be appropriate to say too much, but then I ignored it.

'Farley Johnston, let's get this straight. Don't tell me what to do. Don't presume that just because I have an appropriate conversation with you once, that I will drop everything and come running when you tell me to. I won't. I am actually supposed to be at school right now.' I'd meant to stop at the first bit. And say it not quite as loudly. The woman frowned at me. I'd probably interfered with her Positive Energy or something.

'But you aren't at school; you're here,' he said cheerfully, and he handed me a paper bag before I could qualify my presence.

'What's this?'

'Sit down,' he said, adding, 'Please. Not an order, an invitation. Just to clarify.'

'Thanks for sharing your table,' the man said before he took their empty plates to the counter, and the woman put her coat on.

'My table is your table. Any time.' Was he always this cheesy? I sat though. Only because I was curious about the bag. Maybe I had been right in the beginning, and these were the motivational, self-help books he had been gearing up to sell me in some elaborate sales pitch.

'So, what is this?' I asked again, with a little more sarcasm, now that the frowning lady had left.

'Happy Birthday.'

'What, you're a mind reader now? How do you know it's my birthday?' It was getting harder to be negative though. First Tracey's pictures and now this. I didn't know if I'd ever met someone as happy as Farley always seemed to be.

'I'm not that new age. Social media. I assume you want people to know the info on your page?'

I'd never quite understood what those privacy settings meant. I opened the bag to find a sketch pad, a bunch of pencils — art pencils, all with different numbers, and a box of pastels.

In a way I wanted to take out a pencil, to open the pastels and savour the colours. But this other part of me, the part that made my stomach feel queasy, wanted to throw the bag at Farley.

'You don't seem to think your art is art. Maybe some artist tools will change your mind.'

'You shouldn't have done that.' I wasn't saying it because it was the socially polite thing to say. My parents had spent most of my childhood trying to channel me into some sort of 'interest'. Maybe it was because they couldn't understand how one daughter could be so sure of what she loved, and one so not interested in anything. They had done their best in encouraging me.

But it had always felt like so much pressure. There wasn't anything that I was good at like Emma was good at dancing. No matter how many different classes they enrolled me in. At least the cancer had put a stop to that. Mom didn't hand me flyers and community centre programmes anymore.

Drawing was different. It hadn't felt like an interest I had to 'pursue'. It had just been something I started to do. And it was private, not something I wanted to share with anyone. Farley was ruining that. I didn't want him to be some teacher, or mentor, or something.

But if that was the case, why was I sitting here? I'd specifically come here to ask him to help me choose a camera, hadn't I? Or was that just an excuse to see him?

I was suddenly aware of how close we were sitting. Close enough to recognise the shampoo he'd used this morning, and to see each shade of purple on the stripey hoodie I'd never seen him without. Close enough that if I just shifted a

127

centimetre or two our knees would touch. I kind of wanted to shift that centimetre closer.

I shoved the thought away. Why hadn't I brought my phone with me? Dell was probably still worrying. I couldn't reassure him that we were okay even if I wanted to now. I didn't even know if we were okay. Had I broken up with him? Did I want to?

'Hey, earth to Jane,' Farley said. 'It's a little token. A thanks for being the first interesting person I have met here sort of thing.'

I couldn't stop my heart from doing a little skip at that. When I looked up at him, into those sincere eyes, with the little laugh lines – I knew he meant what he said, even though I knew he was wrong. It was all just a little too sunshine-and-lightish.

'I'm not interesting.'

But for maybe the first time ever, I felt like I might want to be.

'So, you haven't used a camera at all? Not even the one supplied on every phone for two generations?' Farley was looking at me like I had just told him I didn't know how to tell time.

'I'm not completely clueless, but honestly, photography has not been at the top of my priority list. It's not like I've had anything I *want* to remember in my life.' We were outside the store where I had just spent nearly all of my money on a camera that had more buttons and controlly-bits than most cars. I didn't have a clue how to just 'snap a few pictures', as Farley had just suggested.

'It's all about perspective. You just need the right view to see something magical. There is magic and beauty everywhere, all of the time.' He took the camera from me and took what looked like a bunch of random shots, glancing at the screen after each one he took.

'Come here. See what I mean?' He pulled me closer so I could see the photo he'd taken of our footprints in the snow. We'd had to wade through snow up to our ankles to get to the shop. It had been falling too fast for anyone to bother shovelling yet, though it had stopped during the hour it took Farley to ask nearly a million questions before I finally picked a camera. If I'd just had the photo in front of me, I would have guessed the faint trail of footsteps was on the top of Mount Everest or something. The shadow from the tree across the road marched eerily across our human trail.

'Cool picture,' I conceded. 'I wouldn't mind being shown how to take shots like that, but you are seriously going to have to curb all that positive thinking shit if I'm going to spend this much time with you. It's just weird.'

'Tell, you what. Give me an afternoon and see if I don't shift your perspective even just slightly left of pessimism.'

I hate to admit it, but Farley did kind of show me magic that day. He had the weather on his side though. First, the magic snow fall, and then the sun splitting the clouds apart to reveal a blanket of sparkles everywhere. We could have been in the dingiest city in the world and it would have seemed enchanted on that day.

But it wasn't just the weather, and the excitement of having a new toy to play with all afternoon. It was Farley, and it was me, and it was Farley and me together. I can't even really put my finger on what was so great about it. It was just that whenever he talked, I had the perfect thing to say back to him and *everything* he said seemed to be exactly what I had wanted to hear for ages, only I didn't know it because no one had ever talked to me like Farley did. If you don't know what that feels like, you really have to find someone you can be with like that. I guess it is kind of like magic.

We weren't even doing anything I hadn't done most days for ages; just wandering aimlessly around Kendal. Somehow, with the camera and with Farley, it was just ... fun. I would take a few pictures and then flick through them with Farley looking over my shoulder, and then he would point out where I could have centred things better, or adjusted the aperture, to better deal with the dazzling light. The more pictures I took, the more I wanted to take. It was like drawing, only faster.

I didn't even notice that my feet were going numb from walking around in the snow, wearing runners, until I turned the camera on Farley and saw that his feet were even less appropriately protected from the cold. Birkenstocks and socks aren't great winter footwear, even if the socks were thick wool ones.

'I know there's probably a dress code for hippies, but come on, sandals in the winter?'

'As far as I know, the hippie dress code was dropped years ago. No mandatory peace sign t-shirts anymore either. But remember, I haven't got a mother to teach me the basics.'

'Well, don't look at me for how to dress. Everyone has been trying to improve my fashion sense for years. It isn't working.' I unzipped my coat and held out my arms for emphasis. I was wearing what I pretty much wore for as much of the time as I could get away with – plain jeans and a plain grey hoodie. Not a label to be seen. Hair barely brushed, in a loose pony tail and not one bit of makeup. I guess I could blame my appearance apathy on Emma's illness, like I blamed most of my faults; but really, I had never much cared.

Farley just looked at me for a moment, and even though

his expression was serious, I liked that his eyes always seemed to be smiling. I didn't even feel self-conscious like I usually would have if someone else had looked at me for that long.

'You are the quirkiest person I have met, Jane. I don't think you could hide that behind mundane clothes if you tried.'

'It takes one to know one,' I said, as if I were five, and dipped my head to zip my coat so he wouldn't see just how widely I was smiling.

Weekends in our house, when Emma is in the hospital, which seems like all of the time, follow a pretty regular pattern. We have our routine and it doesn't just keep the house from falling down, it keeps us from thinking about what we are missing in our 'life before Emma got sick'.

Here is the thing. People think that when something really bad happens, you will be lost, not know what to do. 'Everything falls apart,' is what people think. But that isn't true at all. Sure, maybe there's a moment or so when you aren't sure what you should do — and I'm thinking here more about when Grandad died, not when Emma was first diagnosed — but it doesn't last. What happens is, you just find a new routine in the chaos. You find a new way to cope. Things are not upside down at all; habits just shift a little sideways.

Instead of running Emma around to dance practices and recitals, Mom started running her around to doctors' appointments. Instead of spending his time in the garage doing some sort of wood working stuff, Dad worked overtime at the mine. Instead of lying around the house moaning about how everyone should get off my back, I got a boyfriend and lay around his house eating bags of potato chips and racing cars on his console. It was all the same, only less.

So when Emma was in the hospital, our new weekend routine kicked in. Dad spent Saturdays at the hospital with Emma, while Mom tried to get the house in some sort of order for the week again. I was supposed to help her. Then Sunday morning we all went to Red River, and I went in to spend time with Emma first, while Mom and Dad went out for breakfast and to discuss whatever it was that 'the kids' were not supposed to overhear. I bet you it's money they talked about. Or lack of it.

The envelopes marked 'urgent' filling the letter box seemed to be multiplying weekly. I tried not to think about those envelopes; they were just another reminder that life was not getting any better. I mean, it wasn't getting any worse either. There weren't any big guys in black showing up at our door to carry away the television.

But if I really thought about it, there probably was a lot to worry about. I knew that it had cost a lot for Mom to do her law degree, though most of it was by distance education.

Even before Emma got sick and Mom couldn't work at all, I had woken up more than once to Mom and Dad discussing how Mom playing solitaire in an office all day wasn't going to pay the bills. Discussing may not be the right word, but you get the picture.

That is the other thing about Bad Things That Happen. It isn't the Bad Thing itself that you think about most of the time. It's all of the little things that didn't seem so bad before, that slowly get bigger and wear you down. But because of the Bad Thing, you can't really stop just carrying on. And the worst thing is that everybody only wants to help you with the Bad Thing, when they can't help you one bit with it. People ask what they can do, but only for the first while, because after you say *oh thanks, nothing really* a few times, they get bored and get on with their lives. But what they want to do is fix the Bad Thing, which is impossible. And what you really need is help with the little things, which are getting bigger, like the paint that continued to peel off our house and the dishes that never stopped piling up in the sink.

Once, when a teacher asked me if there was anything she could help me with, I suggested she give me the answer sheet to the next quiz. I was joking of course, but she didn't think it was so funny. I'm sure it took her ages to work up the courage to even say anything and she was probably expecting me to cry. Then she could have given me a big hug and felt like she had done something.

I'm rambling a bit. I do that sometimes. What I meant to say, was that this weekend was the first weekend in ages that I *noticed* our Weekend Hospital Routine, particularly how utterly boring it had become. Maybe I did notice it before, but I just hadn't been able to find the energy to care.

This weekend was different. I don't know why, but I felt like I could do something about it. After the hospital scene and the horrible necklace thing, I should have felt like crawling into bed and sleeping all day. That's pretty much what I usually did after a reasonably good week.

Maybe Farley was right. Maybe I had just needed to change my perspective to make my life better, because that Saturday seemed to be the best in a long, long time. Even though there wasn't really anything different about it.

Well, my new camera was different. I couldn't believe I hadn't thought of getting one before. I know it sounds completely ridiculous, but looking through a camera window was like seeing the world for the first time. Normally, I see too much. There are too many details in the world — lines and colours and textures and shades and shadows, not to mention how they all form actual things. It's hard to take it all in sometimes. But with a camera, there's a frame around one bit of it. Move the frame, and you have another bit of it. It's like you can create a billion little universes just by shifting that frame.

And then, what you think you saw and froze in a photo,

might be totally different when you download it. After I helped Mom with the chores – and for once I really did do that, two loads of laundry, and both bathrooms cleaned, sort of a peace offering I guess, after embarrassing her so badly during the week – I started to look through the photos I had taken on Friday afternoon.

Farley had given me a photo program to load on my laptop too, so I started to play around with the images. That gave me the tools to create fifty billion more universes. Time just seemed to melt away. One minute it was six o'clock in the evening and the next minute it was four o'clock in the morning.

I wasn't looking forward to waking up after the meagre four hours sleep I was going to get.

Mom was in the kitchen before I was ready for her to be awake. I'd woken up thinking that I must have overslept and that the time on my phone was wrong. I'd went downstairs to check the time there, and it was only seven am, so I thought I'd just have a drink of water and go back to sleep. But when I turned from the sink, there was Mom – up. Too late.

Mom had been kind of quiet with me all the previous day. I guess she hadn't exactly forgotten my tantrum, but she hadn't mentioned it either. To be honest, I'd been too distracted by my own thoughts to really notice.

Now, she gave me a hug before taking the orange juice from the fridge. She knew better than to speak to me yet though. Neither of us are morning people and we had silently agreed years ago to keep any conversation for at least half an hour after first seeing each other. This was probably an even better agreement now that I had barely gone to bed.

Going back to bed now would just be weird, and I felt more buzzy than tired, so I proceeded to make coffee in the machine. Apparently that was just as weird, judging from how elevated Mom's eyebrows became. Okay, I had never drank coffee before, and I actually didn't know how to make it, but I was sixteen now, wasn't that what I was supposed to do? And I needed something to get me through. People were constantly espousing the merits of caffeine for just these kinds of days.

I had drank half a mug of the thickest, blackest, bitterest liquid I had ever ingested, and Mom had read half a Sunday paper before she thought it safe to say anything.

'Jane, I am so, so sorry that your birthday was a disaster,' she said, and I could see that it really *was* killing her. One thing about my mom is that she always means what she says one hundred per cent, which is good when she's saying good things, but doubly guilt-inducing when you are in the bad books. 'I mean, from our end. I hope the night with your friends was fun.'

'It's all okay, Mom,' I said, and even though I shouldn't have meant that, I did. I should have felt hurt and sad; I didn't. It was the most amazing feeling to not feel that, even though there was this part of me that worried I was cheating by not feeling it.

All I could think of was my new camera, but maybe a part of me did want to hurt her because I didn't say a word about it. Instead, I just said, 'Thanks for the money. It was perfect.'

Mom had this strange look on her face, an expression that was kind of frozen between a smile and a grimace. I thought it was probably a good time to exit and get ready for the hospital, before her computer rebooted and decided which it was.

'Hey, sis,' Emma greeted when I entered her room, in the same way she always did, erasing the hurt I'm sure I had inflicted. She hated it when Mom and I fought, and I hadn't exactly said nice things about her either.

'Hey,' I countered.

I sat down, not sure how we were going to fill the time we had until Mom and Dad came back. I was never comfortable in this building, but today it seemed worse. The smell of the hospital was making me feel ill. Was it always this medicinal smelling? It was like the place had been dipped in TCP. I got back up to open the window, but the latch was just there to make it look like an ordinary window, instead of a hospital one designed to keep even the very air inside. It wouldn't budge. I looked around for something to pry it open with. I'm not sure what I thought I would find. It isn't like there were screwdrivers lying around hospital wards.

'Jane, can you stop pacing around, you're making me dizzy,' Emma said.

'I'm not pacing. I'm trying to get you some untainted air.'

I was trying a butter knife from Emma's breakfast tray now. It seemed like the window frame had been painted from the outside or something. I could feel it starting to give.

'I can't believe they fucking forgot!' Emma exploded, just as the knife snapped in two. I'd never heard Emma swear before. I let the piece of knife I still held clatter to the floor.

'Forgot what?'

'Your birthday! I was furious at Mom.'

'Is that what was going on between you and Mom the other day?'

'Jane, they wouldn't have remembered at all if I hadn't shown Mom my present for you.' I held up my wrist, to show her that I had it on.

'I didn't even want to be part of Mom's stupid, last-minute party, but what could I do? I'm kind of stuck here.' Emma was never belligerent. I sat down. 'Is that your present from Mom and Dad anyway?' I had my camera slung over my shoulder.

'Money,' I said. 'I'd say Dad went to the 7-11 ATM on his way home from work. He didn't even pick me up some cheese nachos and a Slurpee to go with it.' I told her about the card with the hand-drawn '16th' on it. It felt weird to talk to Emma this way; weird-normal though. I just wasn't used to her saying anything bad about anyone.

'I'm sorry, Jane,' she sighed, and when she did I swear she looked like she was old – wise-old.

'What are you sorry for?' There was a list forming in my head of reasons *I* should be sorry. I could think of dozens already. But there was never a reason for Emma to feel regretful.

'For stealing every bit of Mom and Dad. For being such a wimp that I can't ever say what I mean.'

I took out the camera and started taking pictures of her. I had that feeling again, like something wasn't quite right. I mean, more than usual. My sister didn't talk like this.

'Strike a pose for me,' I said, sticking out my tongue at her so she would laugh. She didn't.

'You have to listen to me for once, because I swear if I don't tell you this stuff, I'm going to crack up.'

'Tell me what?'

'Do you know what it's like to try to be the daughter Mom

expects me to be, day after day?'

'I kind of only know the opposite,' I said. I really didn't want to hear any of this. I kept moving, snapping pictures of Emma from different angles.

'I'm like her project,' she said, arms crossed across her chest now.

'What do you mean?' *What was she going on about?*

'I've always been her project, but it's worse being her sick project. At first, I guess I *was* that sick little kid who needed her mommy.'

I remembered the first time she had been in the hospital. Mom would have slept in the bed with Emma if the nurses had let her.

'But now, it's like I can't get out of being that little kid.'

'It's highly overrated, growing up.' I kind of knew that I wasn't saying what she wanted to hear, but I also didn't have a clue what I was supposed to do while she told me things I didn't even want to hear about. 'Besides, nobody can do Cute in a Tutu like you can, Emma. You can't just throw that away.'

'Please, Jane.' When I looked over at her there were fat tears rolling down her cheeks, with more poised to follow. She had gone white – even more pale than usual.

'Do you need the nurse?'

'I need YOU.' The words came out as a sob. 'I've lost me before I even get to find me; I can't lose you too.'

'It's okay, Emma,' I tried to hug her, because it seemed to

be the thing to do, even though she was being a little melo-dramatic, but she shoved me away, and angrily wiped her wet cheeks.

'It is not okay.' Her expression was so fierce and intense I couldn't resist taking a picture.

'Would you put that thing away?' she said, before she threw the closest thing at me, which was her stuffed elephant. I threw it back at her harder and then she threw a pillow.

There's nothing like a good pillow/elephant fight to change the mood. It didn't take long to get Emma smiling again. Crisis averted.

I ignored the swirling in the pit of my stomach that was trying to tell me that all I had done was shut her down. What-ever crisis was going on for Emma, I hadn't made it go away. I'd basically told her not to bother me with it.

It wasn't that I didn't want to be there for her. It's just that my feelings were so knife-edge sharp lately and the thought of letting her talk felt dangerous. It was kind of an instinct, to stay away from that, like if I let myself feel for Emma, I wasn't going to be able to stop – and I had this jumpy feeling that if that happened it was going to be bad.

By Monday I had avoided Dell as long as I could. When I

thought about facing him, it made me feel like throwing up. Because I honestly didn't know how I felt. It had always been so easy to spend every spare moment at Dell's – and except for the disaster of a birthday night nothing had changed.

Only – it had. Everything was changing, and the longer I stayed away from Dell, the less real he felt. But nothing else felt totally solid either.

So I lied and I didn't even do it to his face. I sent him a message. SORRY, NOT MYSELF, DELL. LOTS OF FAMILY STUFF GOING ON. YOU KNOW, WITH EMMA. AND EXAMS COMING UP. LOVE YOU, BUT NEED A LITTLE TIME TO SORT IT ALL OUT. I'LL SEE YOU FRIDAY K? PROMISE.

Technically it was all true. There was something up with Emma and Mom. I was pretty sure I had some tests coming up, though I couldn't seem to remember in which subjects. The sorting things out part was completely made up though. I wasn't sorting out one thing.

Lying aside, it felt fantastic to get rid of my guilt by pressing the 'send' button. I'd forgotten how good it was to be free.

I tried to go to classes. I'd woken up feeling full of energy on Monday and ready to make a new start with school. And the two classes I made it to went really well. I'd even caught up on all of my homework for them on the bus in.

The camera took over in the end though. I had chosen a bunch of pictures of Emma that I wanted to get printed and then find a place to hang out and sketch them. Maybe at The Good Earth. Kaitlin seemed to be tolerant of people hanging around all day. Well, Farley anyway. But I think I was starting to be an extension of him.

He wasn't going to be there. He'd already sent me a message to say that he was going to be gone for a couple of days, to meet his dad. His message had made me smile. WISH ME LUCK. OFF TO MEET THE FATHER IN VANCOUVER. I TOLD YOU HOW MUCH HE LIKES 'ALTERNATIVE CULTURE', RIGHT? THINK I SHOULD LOSE THE GUATEMALAN HOODIE? IS THAT A GOOD COMPROMISE? HE'S PAYING FOR THE FLIGHT. SEE YOU WEDNESDAY. He'd sent another one after that. PS. BY 'SEE YOU WEDNESDAY' I MEAN IF YOU WANT TO, NOT 'YOU MUST'. And one more: OH, AND: GO TO SCHOOL. NOT BECAUSE I CARE – IT WAS YOU WHO POINTED OUT THE FACT THAT YOU DO INDEED ATTEND AN INSTITUTE OF LEARNING (THOUGH EVIDENCE WOULD SUGGEST THIS FACT IS QUESTIONABLE).

'You're taking the bus home?' Tracey was sitting behind our usual seat, beside Brenda when I got on.

'Guess I better spend some time studying.' It was what I was telling everyone now. I'd told Mom that I probably wasn't coming into the hospital this week because I was studying for tests. She had seemed to like hearing that. I don't know if it was the thought of me actually applying myself at school, or not having to see me much that made her happy.

Tracey, on the other hand, seemed uncomfortable with seeing me on the home bus. She always shared a seat with me on the way in, and now she didn't know whether to change seats, or stay sitting beside Brenda.

'It's okay. Stay there,' I helped her out. 'I'm going to use the time to get a jump start on memorising math formulas. Exciting times.'

I had sketched twelve pictures of Emma by Wednesday morning. Some were better than others, but when I laid them all out on my bedroom floor I could see that I was getting better. A few of them were particularly good.

It was like there were years of sketching pouring out of me. I couldn't seem to stop now that I had properly started. It didn't even seem strange not to be going to Dell's house every day. I couldn't wait to get home to start drawing.

The only problem was, once I started, I couldn't seem to

stop. It had been five o'clock this morning when I went to bed. But now, at 7:30 am I was wide awake.

I didn't bother going to classes at all on Wednesday. I just went straight to The Good Earth to meet Farley.

'Hello, world traveller,' I said, as I slid into the seat opposite him. It seemed like it had been years, not days, since I had last seen him.

There weren't any books at his table today. And he didn't have on his familiar hoodie. It had been replaced by a checked, button-down shirt. I wasn't sure I liked it.

But the big difference was his smile. Usually, he had this bemused look to him. Today his smile was flat. Not even his eyes were smiling.

I had things to share with him though, so I decided to ignore it. Besides, it wasn't my job to read people's expressions. I wasn't some kind of fortune teller.

He didn't give me a chance to share anything though.

'Can you do something for me?' He wasn't kidding about not liking small talk.

'I doubt it,' I said. 'The last time I was useful to anyone was ... I don't remember it ever happening.'

'Today is the day then,' he said. 'I need a side kick. Moral

146

support. Maybe an excuse to leave in a hurry if it comes to it.'

'Sounds more interesting than going back to school for P.E. Sure, I'll do my best.'

Farley had borrowed Kaitlin's car, which had a couple of glitches. The main one being that it had to be parked on a hill because it wouldn't start until it was rolling in neutral. The other glitch was a very big hole in the passenger side floor. I spent the first few minutes watching the road spin under my feet, until I felt a bit dizzy. Plus I thought I should probably pay attention to where we were going, since Farley had talked about the possible need to make a getaway.

He hadn't actually told me where we were going, but it seemed to be out of town since we were on the highway heading south. I thought of how pleased Mom would be to hear of me getting in the car – especially one with a hole in the floor – with some guy I had only known for less than two weeks, to go to some undisclosed destination. She would have killed me before he had a chance to.

I didn't care. I didn't care about much. What I mean is, this was the first week of my life that I didn't want to care. I'd shifted my frame of reference and suddenly the blank nothingness had switched to endless possibility. I didn't want that marred by worry. It turns out it was pretty easy to just stop it.

'I know you don't feel the need to tell me where we are going,' I said. 'But perhaps you could share the purpose of this journey? You did mention something about moral support. I feel I should get ready for that.'

'Grandparents,' he said. 'We are going to see my grandparents.'

My grandfather had been the reason my family had moved back here from Vancouver. Maybe it was because all of their other parents had died young and he was the only one left. They probably felt a bit like orphans. Maybe that was why Mom was so forgiving of how her dad had abandoned her when she was a kid.

I don't remember much about my life in the city. When you're little, who cares where you live? Your world isn't much bigger than your house and your parents anyway.

I do remember meeting my grandfather for the first time though. Everyone I knew had grandparents when I was five of course. At least one of them. So I'd been a bit of an oddball without any. Until Mom told me that I did have one.

I only got to talk to him on the phone once a week for

the longest time though. And you can keep up any persona on the phone if the conversations are fairly short, which I'm sure they were, since I was five and not exactly great with conversation skills. He seemed wonderful on the phone. I'm sure I embellished the grandparent-like aspects of him in my mind. I remember talking about him all of the time. I'm sure bragging rights came into it, finally having a grandparent to talk about to other kids.

So even if it was a falsehood, I had this specific picture of him, which was completely shattered when I actually got to meet him. I had expected an old man, with maybe a big yellow dog at his feet – the dog being a very important part, because I wanted one so badly, and Emma was allergic. On the drive to his house I just knew he would have presents for us, and every sort of cake on the table, which he would offer out freely.

He was nothing like that. In fact, when he opened the door to his big, old house on the hill behind Kendal, I thought he was someone else and my grandfather was inside, sitting in his rocking chair of course, ready to tell me stories. Instead, he was an ordinary man. Worse really. A stern, older man, who liked children to be seen and not heard.

I think I spent most of that first visit sneaking around the big, old house just to avoid him.

Emma loved him straight away though. She was almost a baby still, and she loved everyone. He loved her straight back.

It wasn't like that with me and Grandad. It took us a long time to even get used to each other, slowly, and I'm not sure he ever really liked me. I don't know how much I liked him either if I'm honest, even though, over the years, I did end up loving him.

Do you know how that is, when you love someone even though you don't like them? You would think the two things, like and love, had to go together, but they don't necessarily. Maybe that is what makes everything so complicated. If I loved Dell, or if I didn't like him so much, things would be easy. If I didn't love Emma so, so much, or if I could just get to like her better, maybe things would be easier with us. It's when there's a dichotomy between like and love that there's a problem.

For never having been to his grandparents' house, Dell had a very easy time finding it. That didn't surprise me. He was pretty smart, probably had the google map printed on his brain. Anyway, it was hardly out of Kendal. I'd had this idea in my head of a road trip – maybe I had watched too many movies. Life wasn't really like that.

We had enough time for him to fill me in on the story though.

'Right. Here is the thing. My grandparents blamed my dad

for my mom dying. They never liked him. And they especially hated him when my mom moved to the commune
and stopped talking to them. They wouldn't have anything
to do with him, or by extension, me, when I showed up
in the world. But now my dad has told them I'm here and
they have found it in their hearts to want to meet their only
grandson.' I think Dell would tell you anything if you asked.
He wasn't afraid of sharing.

'And, was it your dad's fault?' I asked, 'I mean, her dying?'

'Maybe.'

That was not what I expected. I wondered if murder ran
in the family.

'Yes. No,' he went on, and then paused, frowning. 'I guess
that is what I came to find out.'

'That didn't really answer my question, but I'm taking it
he didn't stab her to death or anything.' It was only after
I said it that I thought about how highly inappropriate a
thing that was to say. Luckily, it was Farley I had said it to.
He just laughed, which made his face look much more like
him again.

'No, I'm not on some sort of murder mystery tour,' he
said. 'She had epilepsy. She wanted to breastfeed me and
didn't like the thought of me ingesting the medication she
had to take. Going off it didn't go well. Unfortunately, Dad
wasn't home when it didn't go well.'

'Wow. Didn't see that one coming. You don't really soften

the blows do you?'

'You asked.'

'I thought my mom had the ultimate power to instil guilt, but your mom tops mine. It's like she killed herself for you. Do you feel guilty forever?'

'Jane! You can't go around saying things like that!' he exclaimed, but he had a genuine smile on his face when he said it.

I was going to take my camera in, just in case there was some sort of big fight that made for interesting photography, but Farley was in a particularly conformist mood and wouldn't let me. That meant there was really nothing for me to do but follow along like a dog. For once I wasn't in the middle of the drama though, and it was a lot warmer than walking the streets would be.

There wasn't anything to distinguish their house from any around them. One in a row of bungalows, with wide tarmac drives and precise, perfect flower beds placed strategically in the front lawn. At least my grandfather's house had been kind of a statement – a big Victorian affair, complete with one of those round, tower-like rooms. It's one of the only things that my grandfather and I shared, our love for that house.

You would expect that people who completely shut family members out of their life *would* stand out in some way. If Farley's grandparents stood out in any way though, then they were hiding it well from the outside.

And on the inside. Two sweet looking old people ushered us in to their tidy, neutrally decorated kitchen. They were exactly what my six-year-old self thought grandparents should be. Okay, they didn't have a big yellow dog, but they had an orange cat that weaved in and out of our legs the whole time we were there.

'Come in out the cold, Farley,' the woman greeted, taking his hand in both of hers as if they had known each other all of their lives. 'And who is this?' The question was also warm.

'This is my friend Jane, Ma'am.'

God, he was so American! I hadn't noticed it before. *Nobody* around here would say Ma'am — especially to their grandmother, estranged or not. Not only that, but that cocky, surety that I had come to almost like was gone. His shoulders had dropped just that little and he held his hands clasped in front of him.

She just smiled at his faux pas, but the man who came in to shake his hand and mine didn't let it go.

'Around here, there are no Ma'ams or Misters. If you're not comfortable with Grandma and Grandpa, then it's Bill and Helen.'

'How about Grandpa Bill and Grandma Helen?' I couldn't

seem to keep my mouth shut. I concentrated hard on shutting it now and determined to keep it that way. This was none of my business.

Somehow, instead of offending people like I usually did though, however inappropriate it was, everything I said was the right thing. They all laughed. All of them. Even though Farley did not look comfortable.

'So, your dad says that you are a concert violist, one of the best in Washington State,' Helen said, while she got a tin of biscuits out of the cupboard to go with the hot chocolate she had already poured us. She was doing proper grandmother stuff, and talking to Farley like they were catching up on the latest news, not his whole entire life.

'I like to play,' was all he said. He could have perhaps filled me in on this fact. I wondered what else he had kept.

'We like a spot of music here too,' said Bill, and he went to put the radio on, tuning it to the classical station for Farley.

The conversation pretty much went on like that. It was nice, polite talk. Friendly even. I got a little bored, but like I said at least it was warm, and the biscuits and hot chocolate were great.

Plus, I was learning a bit more about Farley too, stuff he probably wouldn't have shared with me. He had graduated from high school early – skipping grades apparently. No wonder the titles on his textbooks were practically Greek to me. They were probably something like third-year college books. Maybe it was good that I hadn't known these things before. I probably would have avoided him like the plague. It was bad enough having a child prodigy in the house, without having one as a friend as well.

About an hour had gone by when the phone rang and Bill went to answer it.

'That will be Joe,' Helen said, like we knew who Joe was. Sure enough Bill was back in a minute or so with, 'That was Joe. He needs us to drive him in for his groceries.'

'Joe is our neighbour,' Helen enlightened us. 'He broke his ankle a few weeks ago, falling on the ice during that bad cold snap. He says he doesn't need any help – except to drive him everywhere!'

Bill was already putting on his coat that was at the ready on the back of his chair.

'Well, we better get a move on. Joe will have us driving all over town before the afternoon is finished.'

'Do you need a ride in, loves?' asked Helen.

'No, we borrowed a car M—' Farley stopped himself in time.

'We are so sorry to have to rush off like this, but Joe has us run off our feet,' she said. I noticed that Bill didn't add to the apology.

'Oh, we understand,' I said, yet again opening my mouth. I kind of had to, because Farley was deflating in front of me. I don't think the grandparents noticed though.

'We would love to have you back any time at all,' Helen continued.

'Great to meet you, Son,' Bill said, gripping Farley's hand once again.

'You too,' Farley managed.

And then we were kind of ushered out the door. They stood on the steps waving as we got into the car, their door locked behind them. I thought that Farley would want to get away as fast as he could, but he sat behind the wheel, shoulders hunched forward.

'We can't go, Jane.'

'Listen, it was a first meeting. They aren't going anywhere. You can go back another time. Have a proper talk with them,' I tried to rationalise. He was right though. It was how I would feel if they had been my grandparents. He was leaving before barely even meeting them. He didn't even have solid plans to come back again. They were nice, but too nice – and the worst part was he didn't know one more thing about his mom.

There had not been a single mention of her, which was weird. I hadn't even seen a picture of her on any wall or shelf. It was like they were pretending that everything had always been fine, that she had never existed, which I pretty much doubted was how they really felt. If that was Mom and Dad twenty years from now, if Emma …? I didn't want to think about that.

And this Joe story? I didn't believe one word of their excuse to leave. I think if it were me, I would have told Joe his groceries could wait; I was meeting my grandson for the first time.

'Hey, here I am for the moral support,' I tried, since he still hadn't moved. 'Let's get out of here before Bill and Helens' smiles freeze on their faces.'

'No, really, we can't go,' Farley insisted. 'I forgot to park on a hill, and there's no way I am pushing the car with those two watching.'

'Take out your phone,' I said.

'What?'

'Just take out your phone and pretend that you are talking to someone. Trust me.'

Farley took out his phone and looked at it helplessly. Bill and Helen were still standing on their front steps. 'Hello, Dad. Oh, you really need to talk to me right now?' I prompted him. He lifted the phone to his ear and started to move his lips silently, while I hopped out of the car and marched back up to the house.

'Farley just got a call from his dad, so he has to take it,' I lied. 'You may as well head off, because it's a call that might take a little while.'

Helen looked at Bill, and I could see the questions playing in his head. What, did he think his own grandson was going to rob him if they left before us?

'Look, I know it's going to be a long call, because his dad was really worried about him coming here. Farley has this complex about rejection. You know, having his mom die on him, and then having grandparents who didn't want anything to do with him. He's been in therapy for years over it. His dad is going to want to talk to him for a while to make sure he is okay.'

I kind of knew I had gone a bit overboard because both of their mouths were wide open. It worked though. When I stopped talking, they both just nodded and walked to their car as quickly as they could. They had driven down the drive before I even got back to the car.

'What did you say to them?' Farley asked, putting his phone down.

'Oh, nothing much,' I said. 'How is your dad anyway?'

'You really are nuts, you know that don't you?'

'You are the one talking to the stars, Farley. I am grounded in practical, every day grandparent-scaring techniques.'

He still looked a bit shell shocked.

'It could be worse. They could have invited us along to ferry Joe around.'

You know when you look at someone, and you just *know*

that you are thinking the same thoughts and feeling the same feelings? When Farley looked at me, when our eyes met, I knew that we were on the same wavelength. And there was a spark. If we had been in a cheesy movie, I suppose this would have been when we kissed – but we weren't and so we ended up in a fit of hysteric laughing instead, which, for now, was just as good.

Kaitlin wasn't expecting the car back for a while, but once we finally stopped laughing, and had the car running, which took quite a few attempts, pushing it until we could find some sort of a slant on the tarmac drive, I couldn't think of anywhere we could go.

'There isn't exactly much to do around here,' I said, stating the obvious. I've pretty much told you what Kendal is like – picture any small town, with a little park and a river and your usual shops. Okay, there's a skating rink if you're into that, or the cinema – but it's only open on weekends. And then you've got the outskirts, like this, with nothing but houses with half-acre lawns – and nothing but the highway to connect them.

'What do you mean?' Farley countered. 'Look out that window. You have whole mountains as playgrounds.' He swept his arm in a slow-motion arc, and my eyes were drawn to the mountains behind the houses, that he obviously wanted me to see. Okay sure; they were probably spectacular to look at – if you hadn't spent most of your life seeing them. I didn't see what there was to do, even if you went that far though.

'Just supposing tromping through the woods was my thing – and it isn't – November is not exactly the month to do it,' I said. We were getting close to town, and even though the morning had been a bit weird, I didn't want it to end. I tried to think of somewhere we could go, something we could do.

'I could save you the bus ride to Red River,' he said. 'You could introduce me to your sister.'

Damn it. I *really* had to change the privacy settings on my profiles. So much for having something of my own. I didn't want to talk about Emma. I didn't know until then, until he had ruined it, how good it had been to have one person who didn't think about her every time they saw me.

'So, did it make for good browsing last night, Farley? Did you check out the YouTube video her dance classmates put together to raise funds? How about the Facebook page my parents' friends thought was such a great idea. Notice anything? She's ten in every picture, every dance video. Well, guess what? She isn't ten anymore. And it isn't cute anymore. It isn't even sad anymore. It is mind-numbingly never ending.'

Five minutes ago I had been laughing so hard my ribs still hurt, and now I was so angry I could spit. 'So if you are looking for some star to hang your do-gooding hat on, you can look elsewhere.' I turned away, so irate I didn't even want to see him.

Neither of us said anything for the rest of the drive. He had ruined it and then I had made sure it couldn't be fixed. Now I was not only angry at Farley's voyeurism, but I was sick at the thought of losing the one interesting thing in my life.

Farley parked the car in the spot he had collected it from. I was about to get out and walk away, when he took my hand and laced his fingers between mine. The anger melted. I wanted to hold his hand forever.

'You met my grandparents; I kind of just wanted to meet someone in your life,' he said, and I could see that he had recovered from the visit now. He was wearing his calm, sure expression again. 'Maybe you have a cat or a dog for me to meet? A pet might be a safer bet.'

One thing about not going to the hospital or to Dell's house was that I was seeing more of Dad. At first, I wasn't sure that was a good thing. Here is the thing; my dad is probably my favourite person in the world. I know that doesn't sound like a very cool thing to say, but it's true. He is the calm in our family, the one who never seems to get riled by anything. He has this way of making me feel like everything is okay.

That's how he was before anyway. But now, he is just ... not really there anymore. Maybe it's that he is tired. I don't know. Or maybe it's that it's mostly just me and him in the house, and without Mom's hyper vigilant lookout for anything that isn't perfect, his calmness just ends up being nothingness. All I know is that I had been so tired and bored myself, and when I was around Dad it just made me feel even more like that. Like together we couldn't find one bit of happiness. Somehow it made everything worse to see him like that.

But since I was home more when he walked in the door, instead of coming in when he was nearly asleep, it seemed like we had more to talk about. Well I did anyway, and he was more awake to listen to it.

'Lasagne is in the oven and the coffee is just brewed,' I said when Dad slumped through the door at six o'clock that evening. My coffee making skills had improved, and I was finding that if I started to drink it early in the evening, I could sketch half the night and still feel great in the morning. I took his parka before he draped it over a chair arm like usual. He settled into his favourite chair to watch the news, while I got us each a big cup of coffee.

'So you didn't go to the hospital again today?' he asked, as

I handed him his cup.

'Catching up on school work,' I said quickly before I moved on to more truthful topics. 'Did you know that there are forty-three muscles in a human face? Think of the infinite possible expressions you can make by combining those muscles in different ways.' I demonstrated a few of those expressions for Dad, and he actually laughed.

Farley had suggested I do a little studying of bones and muscles, if I was interested in drawing people. He'd lent me an anatomy book, but I preferred to surf through websites, finding out interesting facts, like that one.

'There's some controversy about whether expressions are universally the same, or whether they're culturally learned. I have been checking out some YouTube clips to see which side of the fence I am on with that one.'

Dad was looking kind of dazed. I suppose it was a bit of a shift for him, from falling asleep in a heap every evening, to listening to my scintillating conversation.

'Have you watched any of those Bollywood movies, Dad? Did you know that India produces double the movies that Hollywood produces?' I remembered that I needed to put the garlic bread in the oven. 'Back in a sec, Dad.'

'Do you want to see some more of my photos?' I asked, coming back in the room. He had been kind of interested the night before, but tiredness had taken over before he could get through half of them.

'Yes, but only if you sit down, Jane. I'm just too tired for all of this bouncing around the house.'

'I'm not bouncing. I'm happy,' I said.

'There's happy, and then there's happy."

'Of course there is,' I retorted. 'And all of it's good.' It was, wasn't it? So why did Dad's questioning make me feel so defensive?

We were sitting at Farley's usual table. I was trying to claim half of it, shifting his pile of obscurely titled texts to one of the chairs, hanging the violin case on the back of another chair, so that I could make room for my sketch pad.

'So, are you ever going to play me that thing?'

'The way you say that makes me highly sceptical you'd be an appreciative audience,' he said, still trying to read the book in front of him.

'You could be right,' I said. I had this picture of Farley in a suit, with a bow-tie, sitting with an orchestra. It kind of ruined the image in front of me. I was warming to his layered, woolly look. It suited him.

'I like the way I can always count on you to give me straight up honesty, Jane.' *I* liked the way he never seemed offended by it.

'But, then again I could be impressionable when it comes to music. I basically only know what I hate.' I thought of the stuff Dell liked — actually what most people I knew liked; I'd never understood how anyone could feel passionate about any of it.

'That makes me even more sure that you don't need to hear me play.' He turned a page in his book, eyes still down.

'Still, it only seems fair. You've basically forced me to show you my art. Don't you think you should show me yours?'

'Fine.' He sighed, and closed the book he had been trying to read. He shouted over to Kaitlin, who was at her usual station behind the counter. 'Throw me your keys will you? I need a studio space to serenade Jane in.'

Farley had to warm the car up before he could play, which also gave him time to figure out how he was even going to make space to play in Kaitlin's miniature car. He'd moved the front seats right up, so he could stretch his lanky self out in the back seat. That meant I was squished into the remaining space in the passenger seat.

'You're sure you want to hear this? I'm pretty sure you are going to hate it.' For just a moment I saw — felt it more than I saw it — his trepidation.

'How bad can it be? You're one of the best aren't you?'

'Okay. Let's just do this.'

What he played was good; I could tell it was good even though the only classical music I knew was from the radio station my mom listened to – the same one my Grandad had listened to. I'd never paid much attention to it. You couldn't help but pay attention when Farley played though. It was pretty stunning, in a way that almost scared me. He seemed to have absolute control over every note, like each one was held on the strings until he launched it in precisely the direction he wanted it to go. As he played, his face mirrored that precision, every muscle taunt, his eyes intensely focused on some spot in his mind where he controlled the notes.

When he stopped, I didn't know what to say. There weren't any words for what I had heard. Farley saved me by speaking first.

'I don't know what I'm going to do with this.' He lifted the violin from his knee and laid it back down. His face was back to being Farley, only a little sad. I didn't know how he could be sad about being able to play like that.

'What do you mean?'

'Nothing makes my dad happier than me playing this music. Do you know what that's like?'

I shook my head. I didn't, but his question sounded uncomfortably like Emma's plea for me to listen to her.

'What would you do, if you didn't want to do it anymore?'

Farley asked. It wasn't a rhetorical question. He was looking at me like I had an answer.

'Do what?' I asked.

'This – play classical violin. But it isn't only about me. I don't just do this in my spare time. I've trained for years, and the week before I came here I was offered a place in the Boston Symphony Orchestra.'

'That's a good thing isn't it?' As supportive as I was trying to be, it didn't sound like a good thing for me.

'It should be, but it doesn't feel like it.' Farley said. 'I've been delaying my decision, but they won't wait much longer. Should I go?'

'Play me something you love,' I blurted, not wanting to honestly answer his question about what he should do.

'How do you know I didn't love that?' he asked.

I did know, but it took me a minute to think of how I could articulate how I knew.

'When I draw a sketch that I end up loving, I feel it, from a place where there isn't thought. It's like … I'm not in control.' Somehow, it seemed okay to talk like this with Farley. 'What you played was …' I searched for the right words. 'It was incredible, and perfect, but I didn't feel it. You didn't feel it.'

Farley just stared at me, his mouth open. I was afraid my honesty had gone too far this time.

'Nobody knows that. *Everybody* else feels it.'

'Maybe they want to, because it's obviously that good. Seriously though, Farley. You don't get that good randomly. You love something about this – so show me what it is.' It was weird; with Farley I just trusted my gut that I knew what he felt, what he meant. I could say these things without being afraid he would look at me like I had two heads.

'Okay. I've been playing around with Irish fiddle tunes. God, my dad would kill me – all those lessons, all of that classical training going to waste … I've just been listening to tunes and playing what I like, figuring them out by ear. The patterns are simple, but even so, I'm not that good yet.'

'Show me.'

You know when you see someone you really care about, doing something they love? It's like all of the best things about them are suddenly visible, where they weren't before that. And you know *this* – *this* is exactly why you love them, this thing that you can't even articulate, but you recognise immediately.

It was exactly like that to see Farley play the music he loved. His eyes were closed, but even so I could tell his eyes were smiling in that most Farley way. His whole posture was soft and fluid, just like he walked when he wasn't caring who was watching him.

I don't know one thing about Irish music, but it was like everything Farley loved about it was contagious. He kept playing for about ten minutes; his fingers, those beautifully slender fingers, flying, pressing each string with such ease, and the bow almost singing. The music was just like Farley, it was so incredibly optimistic.

And then he switched and played this really slow music, with all of these little slips of notes that looked just like tiny flowers in my mind. It was so beautiful and sad.

I tried to hide behind the seat to wipe my eyes, so Farley wouldn't see he'd made me cry. It seemed so sappy to be sobbing over music. My voice gave it away though. It was a little wobbly.

'You need to keep playing that, Farley.'

'It isn't that easy, Jane.' I didn't like the way his eyes lost all mirth when he said it.

'How can you be all 'trust-in-the-stars' and not know in your heart that it really is that easy.' I'd never heard music that could make me cry.

'I thought you didn't believe any of that?'

'I don't. My straight-up, no bullshit, assessment brings me to exactly the same conclusion as your 'trust in the stars' in this case.' It was true, but I couldn't help thinking that I'd just heard music that was nothing less than magic.

PRESTO PATETICO

'VERY, VERY FAST, WITH GREAT EMOTION'

The weekend came too soon. Something was happening to time. It was moving too quickly. I was used to it barely moving, and now here it was the weekend and I wasn't ready for it. It had been such a good week. But now it was 'D Day'. 'D' for Dell.

For once, on the ride home I could have done with some mindless chatting with the girls, but none of them were on the bus. Tracey had been meeting her mom, and Brenda and Aishling were hanging out in town.

I needed something to stop me from thinking about having to see Dell. It made me feel sick to my stomach just thinking about it.

Today was the day I was supposed to go back to him. And I just couldn't.

I didn't go see Dell. I didn't even ring him or message him. I left a message on the table to tell Dad that I had the flu and that I just needed to sleep. It was sort of true. I sort of felt ill. Only I didn't sleep. I just kept quiet when he came in. It was easy to do that. Pencils don't make any noise.

'I still really don't feel well,' I said to Mom when she got up on Sunday morning. I almost believed it myself I was getting so good at being sick. She had let me 'sleep' all Saturday afternoon. I'd made a brief appearance for dinner, and it had been easy to not eat anything. Food was kind of making me feel ill lately. Maybe I really was sick.

People were kind of making me feel ill too. People required talking, which required thinking, and all I wanted to do was not think. I wanted to draw. There were so many images, and not enough time.

'Maybe you should stay home today, Jane,' she indulged me. 'You are looking quite pale. Probably better to stay away from Emma if you aren't well.'

I nodded. For once I was glad that she thought of Emma before me.

'Dell is worried about you,' Tracey said when I got on the bus on Monday. I hadn't told Tracey anything about my birthday, or that I had told Dell that I didn't want to see him for a week. Or that I hadn't seen him again this weekend. I was trying not to think about it. He had tried to ring me a couple of times; I'd turned the volume to mute so I didn't have to decide whether to answer when he rang.

'Is he?' I said, trying to look surprised, like there was no problem at all. 'Did you run into him?'

'Not exactly,' she said. She hesitated a moment, doing that thing where she bites her lip when she wants to talk, but can't. 'He. Well. He wanted to just talk to you, but you wouldn't answer.'

'Oh, yeah I know I missed a couple of calls from him. Studying has been crazy.' I kind of forgot that this was Tracey I was talking to, who knew that almost anything could distract me from studying. 'Can you believe I just said that?'

I started to laugh, but Tracey didn't. She was still looking at me in complete seriousness, which made me feel strange. She was right. I knew it wasn't funny what I was doing to Dell, but I still couldn't *feel* that.

'Jane, you have missed dozens of calls from him and not rang him back once.'

It didn't seem like he had called that much. Obviously Tracey had a more accurate count than me though.

'I'll talk to him. I really will.' I wanted the conversation to just end. I had been looking forward to showing Farley my newest sketches, which I had worked on all weekend, and I didn't want thoughts coming into my head that would ruin that.

It was just so good to feel happy for once, but maybe because it had been so long since I had felt that way, it got ruined too easily. It was like I was walking this ridge, on top of the world, sun shining, but the path was so narrow that anybody only had to give me a little yank and I would tumble back into the dark of feeling nothing on one side, or into the fireworks of horrible feeling on the other side.

'He's really having a hard time, Jane. It doesn't make any sense.'

'I know, alright!' There, she had ruined it. 'Can I not have one bit of peace for a week or two? Do you think that it is too much to ask for? Why does everyone think this is a bad thing?'

Now I had ruined it as well, because Tracey was blinking back tears as fast as she could. And even though I desperately wanted to feel bad – there was nothing but this anger.

The pictures saved me. Pictures in my mind. All of the photographs I had taken over the last few days started to come into my head and they pushed out any thought. Any thought that wasn't about the images. Pictures of Emma, of the trees in the park, of Farley driving, of Dad asleep, of our house, of my room, of the streets of Kendal, of Farley's grandparents' house, taken between pushes of the car, of my grandfather's house.

That one I hadn't taken. There was no way I was going back there ever again. Where had that picture come from?

But now I couldn't stop the images. They kept coming. Every time I blinked, a new picture, like the digital photo frame Mom kept on the mantelpiece, that wouldn't stop flipping to a new picture, even when you just wanted to look at that last one a little longer.

I closed my eyes tight, trying to stop the slide show, silently cursing Tracey and willing with all my might for that happy feeling to return.

Kaitlin was at her usual station when I walked in, leaning over the counter, staring out the window like it might bring customers in. I got the nod. She wasn't much of a talker, but that was okay. She'd never once made me feel like I shouldn't be there either, even when I didn't have any money to buy anything, which was most of the time. I vowed that when I had money I would keep coming here and spend every penny I had on weird bread and healthy drinks.

'You know that you are exactly the bad influence that my father fears I will fall under, don't you?' Farley greeted.

'Me? A representative of the hard-working, traditional-values contingent around here?'

'I'm referring more to the frequency of which you are *not* in school.'

'Oh, that,' I dismissed, though I did feel a slight flutter of guilt rising. I swallowed it down. 'No time. You need to teach me how to get my houses to stop looking like they were built by Dr Seuss.'

'See, here you are, distracting me from my own studies.' He sighed dramatically and closed the text he had open in from of him. 'And I was just at a really good part.'

'Okay, show me where the problem is?'

The happy feeling was coming back now that I was sitting across from Farley, sketch pad between us. He looked at each sketch like it was some sort of Mona Lisa – which none of them were, especially since I couldn't seem to get the perspective right. I noticed that Farley was wearing his glasses again. They did give him a slightly less cool look, but I liked it. Geeky cute you might say, only not quite geeky enough, and a little too pretty to be cute. I sat on my hands to stop them from reaching up to touch that pretty face.

My phone beeped. And beeped again. I ignored it until the fourth beep and then pulled it out of my pocket in annoyance. Annoyance and a tiny sliver of worry. I didn't like it when Emma was in the hospital. What if I didn't check my phone, and something had gone wrong?

Dell had given up on ringing me. He was messaging me now. He never communicated through writing if he could get away with it so the messages were short. U OK, CALL ME JANE and even U NO I LOVE YOU – not even 'luv', but 'love'. And finally PLEASE.

Could he not leave me alone? Why was he hassling me like this? First Tracey had to remind me that I hadn't rung him, and now here he was bothering me himself. White hot anger rose, and I couldn't stop it.

'Jane?' Farley looked a little startled. 'Are you okay? I don't think I would like to be the sender of that message, based on that look on your face. You could slay a dragon with a flash of that scowl.'

'Have you been to Verwood yet?' Everything that was wrong with Dell suddenly converged in one image.

'Really. Are you okay, Jane?'

'Sometimes you would think you were stepping back in time when you walk down the street there, except that there's a double-cab 350 parked in every drive instead of a horse. We have this one restaurant, this one pub, this one gas station – and kind of attached to it is this one store. It never has anything in it that you need. Like, if Mom would send me for a can of kidney beans, they would only have baked beans that day, and the next day, if Dad wanted baked beans they would only have kidney beans.' The words kept coming. 'But even though they never have what you need, they have all of these things that you would never need. Or maybe someone might have needed or wanted it in say, 1920, maybe before they could just get in the car and drive to Kendal or Red River. So some of the stuff has been there forever. Not just groceries, but weird things like ornaments and fishing gear and makeup. Well, maybe the makeup is recent enough.'

'Jane, breathe.' Farley had his hand on my arm, and I so wanted to think of that, but I couldn't stop yet.

'They also have a little section of jewellery. Mostly really tacky stuff for tourists. You're American, you know the stuff tourists would think is Canadian. Gold nuggets on a chain, silver dream catcher earrings, bracelets with turquoise stones. That sort of thing. We don't even *have* turquoise around here. Isn't that Navaho or something?'

'Whoa, where are we going with this exactly?'

'Where we are going with this, is this is the place where Dell got my birthday present – my medal, his medal really. That is as far as he went – two steps from his work. That is as far as he can imagine me. That is why I can't ring him back.' I could see Dell, running in on his lunch break, asking Teresa behind the till to put some sort of present together for me.

'I'm not really sure I understand the whole medal part, but the not ringing him sounds hopeful for me. Seriously though, is that all he did, not get you the right present, for you to be this mad?'

Farley's hand was still on my arm and I had this sudden urge to pull him toward me. He felt real in a way that Dell never had. *I* felt real.

'I'm not mad at him,' I said, only just now recognising that this was true. How could I be mad? Dell couldn't help that

Verwood practically defined him; the small-town boy in the small town. And that wasn't a bad thing either; it's just that … it wasn't me. It wasn't me, and Dell didn't even get that.

'I'm sorry, Farley, I have to go.' I pulled my arm away and started to shove my sketch pads back in my bag. I needed to go before I lost my nerve. I knew now what I had to do.

'Are you mad at me?' I looked up at Farley. This wasn't banter. It was real concern. His cracks were showing, insecurity leaking out.

No, Farley, I am afraid I may be mad ABOUT you. That's what I thought. What I said instead was, 'How could I be mad at you? All that peace and love floating around you.' I took one of my sketch pads though, one that was full, and slid it across the table. 'Hold on to that, will you, so you can tell me what I need to learn to be better. Tomorrow.'

I hoped that *I* would know what I needed to be better by then. The buzzy, happy feeling I had welcomed was beginning to feel ominously more buzzy and less happy.

'Jane, are you coming today?' I'd never liked talking to Emma on the phone. It wasn't just that we didn't really do conversation; it was that without seeing her face I could never be sure that I wouldn't say something to upset her too much. Not that I had been doing such a great job of restraining myself in person lately.

'Well, I'm not sure yet. I've a few more tests.' I hadn't gone to the hospital again on Tuesday, and the sick and study excuses wouldn't hold up much longer. The truth was, I hadn't made it to many classes at all. I'd had too much to do, trying to catch up on learning how to draw. I'd had the most fantastic week, and now it was just . . . hard to make myself go back to the usual. It didn't feel right now.

'That's what you said last week, Jane.'

'Yeah, well, I don't exactly schedule the exams. Some of us actually have to go to school.' I let the anger hang there for a minute. I hated it, but I couldn't seem to *not* feel it. If I didn't deal with Dell soon I was going to explode.

'I get it,' Emma finally said.

'Do you?'

'I just . . . it's just that I wanted to talk to you.'

'Talk away.'

'No, not on the phone. Here.'

I could almost see the bad feeling rising, twisting in black swirls up through my intestines, swallowing the bright colours of hope that had been trying to bloom there.

'What's the point anyway?' I continued, and with every word, the blackness advanced. 'You and Mom don't need me there. I am invading your private, little world aren't I? It's not like I belong there one bit. You know what; I don't want you to belong there either. Emma, you have to get out of there. They have to let you out. I can't do it anymore.'

'Are you okay, Jane?' When did Emma get old enough to ask me that? And why did people insist on asking me that, just when I was more okay than I had been in three years. I was wasn't I? I just needed to deal with Dell. It was eating at me. I just needed to do that and everything would be perfect. Well, as perfect as it could be anyway.

I meant to ring Dell. I really did. I was even going to just go and see him. But one minute it was six o'clock, and the next minute it was two o'clock in the morning, with not even much drawing to account for the time gone. Something was happening to the time.

History is not a terrible first period. Generally, we are at least discussing places and times that are not here. I like that.

Also, history teachers really like it when you can spew back dates at them. If you put up your hand to answer, for example, that the Canadian Railway was completed on

November 7th in 1885, you are golden. A history teacher will assume that you know everything if you can give her that date. And I am good with numbers, and dates are essentially numbers. I have gotten away with knowing very little else but dates and time lines.

Usually.

Today, I slid into first class, opened my text, and got ready to spew a date or two before tuning out completely for forty minutes. I had to pace myself. I had to put in at least a three class day today. It was ages since I had.

It should have registered with me that I was in trouble when nobody else took out a textbook. I wouldn't have even noticed but Ms McGuire was late, so I had time to look around, and everyone around me had a pen in their hand, but nothing else. The keener students had another two pens on the desk in front of them. Almost everyone was sitting up straight, not slumped in their chairs like they usually were.

When Ms McGuire finally did come in, with a handful of stapled booklets, I knew it wasn't going to be a good day.

Okay, here is the truth. My system isn't just a system for avoiding school; it's also a system for making sure that I never get less than a C. I miss assignments, I make them up, I do enough on the bus to keep up, and I skip the classes that aren't that important. There's surprisingly little that you have to do to get by if you just figure out what is essential and what is not. Teachers won't tell you that shit of course, but if they think a student's sister might tank it any day, they cut her some slack; they let her in on some of the secrets.

So maybe I wasn't as completely out of control as I seemed. I kind of wanted to be, but I was also kind of too scared to be.

Today was different. I honestly did not know that we had a major test until the papers were put on each of our desks. My mom tells me that she still has dreams of forgetting that she has registered for a class, and then having to write an exam having never been to a single lecture. She thinks it comes from being in school for so long, that she never really stopped being a student at heart.

I don't know about that, but I can tell you that the feeling in real life is as terrifying as any nightmare. There was not a single question that seemed like something I had heard anything about. It was worse though, because I couldn't stop going over and over in my mind, searching for how I possibly missed that there was a test scheduled for today. It felt like I was in some kind of weird fog, where I couldn't move, couldn't remember before yesterday. And then when I tried to think of other classes, to anchor myself, thinking maybe it was just this class; I couldn't think of a single thing that had happened in any of my other classes.

It wasn't until the guy who sat across the aisle looked at me strangely that I realised that I'd just been sitting there while everyone else was furiously writing. I flipped the pages back to the beginning, but when I tried to read the first question, I couldn't concentrate enough for the words to make sense.

What subject was even next? I couldn't remember my timetable! Everyone around me kept writing as fast as they could, and the more I tried to flip through the pages, to remember anything, the more I panicked. I knew there were tricks. I knew I could do the multiple choice questions and the matching section and get at least a few points by default. But I couldn't concentrate enough to read the directions. The words kept jumping around on the page.

The place was so quiet that I could hear my own thoughts booming through my brain, repeating phrases *WHEN DID IT ... HOW DO WE KNOW ... WHAT DO YOU THINK? What did I think? What did I think?* I couldn't think.

'Will you stop it!' the guy across from me whispered. It took me a second to realise that I'd been tapping my pen on the desk. I don't think I was doing it quietly either.

I looked up at Ms McGuire at the front of the room, but she hadn't even noticed. She was reading a book. Couldn't she see that the test didn't make sense? Couldn't she tell that she had picked up the wrong test? Everybody else just kept writing; they didn't know either. They had cheated; they had all seen last year's test, they were answering those questions, but they didn't know that this one was different. Only I knew; but I couldn't do anything about it.

I counted to two hundred, hoping this panic would pass,

and when it didn't I almost ran to the front of the class, thrusting my empty paper at the teacher. I seemed to have startled her, because she looked a bit shocked, but I didn't stop to think about that. I just turned and counted my steps out of the class – willing myself to walk, to not run.

There was a bathroom right beside 212A, which is the room I took history in, and I have never been more thankful for a bathroom in all of my life. As soon as I opened that door, it felt like I was back in my mind. I stood at the sink, hands shaking, looking at a face that slowly became my own. Slowly. At first I couldn't register who it was. I didn't like the face. She terrified me with her demon eyes and pale skin. And then, blink by blink, frame by frame, the face became me and it was okay.

Obviously, I couldn't stay in school, even though I had resolved to be there for the morning. I was slightly freaking myself out. As soon as I left the building though, I felt a hundred times better, which was a thousand times better than I had felt during the history exam. I wasn't going crazy; I was just tired. I had missed reminding myself about the test because I was tired. I hadn't really slept properly for, how long? I didn't know.

Walking helped. It wasn't even that cold today. I could keep walking and I would keep feeling better. It was like coming out of a nightmare. Cold was even good. Well, it was better since I had remembered mittens today. Small things are good.

By the time I had reached the main street I had a plan. Ten laps. Ten laps of the five blocks by five blocks that made up Kendal. I wasn't sure that five by five fully encompassed the town, but it was a good workable number. Five by five was twenty five by ten was two hundred and fifty. A good goal to aim for. A measurable goal.

I only made it one lap before I started to feel panicked again. How had I forgotten it, that exam? I had known it was coming up. I tried to remember what day it was. Friday. How hard was that?

But what had I done on the weekend? I didn't remember seeing Emma. I'd been sick, hadn't I? I had been sick so I didn't need to see Dell, or Emma, or anyone. But I hadn't slept. There had been too many pictures in my head to do that.

The buzzing was back and I couldn't think. Nothing would stick. I was trying to grab thoughts and make them stay. Even a bad thought. Just stay. 'Stop bouncing', 'Sit down, you are making me dizzy', 'Too much energy'. Too much, too much, too much, too much.

My phone. I took it out and messaged the only person I could even hope to save me.

I tried to concentrate on breathing while I sat on the bus, waiting for Farley to save me. He'd told me to get on the bus; that he would be there.

I took out all of my books and laid them on the seat beside me, and then put them all back in my bag again. Where was the bloody day planner? It had my timetable in it. I shuffled through all of my binders and texts looking for it, and then went through my bag again, finding it behind a lunch bag that smelled ominously like oranges gone bad. When I opened to my timetable though, I didn't feel any better. There, in colour coded order, was what my week – every week since September – looked like. Every Friday was history, then English, then P.E. Still, looking at the day, it seemed no more familiar. It was like my own life was just evaporating.

I shoved the book back behind the rotten orange. I didn't want to see the thing. It just made me feel scared, with its concrete proof of how out of control my life was. Instead, I took out my history binder and opened up to a blank piece of paper and started to draw.

Farley bounded up the steps, violin case slung over his shoulder. I felt like crying I was so relieved to see him.

'I'm here,' he stated simply as he sat down beside me.

'You are.' It was more like a sigh than it was a statement.

Just seeing him made me feel better. I was afraid to say much though. My thoughts seemed all jumbled up, and I wasn't sure I could get out words that made sense. So I didn't say anything. I just kept drawing.

Only with Farley could I do this without being afraid of looking crazy, which was ironic since I was feeling the sanest I had all day. He didn't say a word; just put his arm around me. And I let him.

When I put my head against his chest I could feel his heart beating, steady, steady, steady, and his breaths slow, slow. I tried to slow my breathing down to match his, tried to shut out any thoughts, any pictures. Think of breathing, think of breathing. Inhale, exhale, inhale, exhale. Blood, everywhere. A picture exploded in my mind. I knew it all too well. Shit. I didn't want it there. I'd kept it away. I'd refused it entry.

'I found my grandfather dead in his house. He shot himself.'

'Ok.' It was like I had told him I'd had toast for breakfast.

Inhale, exhale, inhale, exhale. The slide show in my head would not move from that picture. Where had it come from? I could see it, I knew I had been there, but I couldn't feel anything about it. It was like something you see posted on some news site.

'Do you think we should get off the bus and call, I don't know, the doctor or someone?' Farley asked finally when I didn't say anything more.

I sat up and started to laugh. And Farley's expression, trying to stay calm and supportive, made me laugh even more. I couldn't stop.

'Not today, you numbskull!' Grandad had been dead for nearly a year. It wasn't a day my family talked about, not because of how he died, because we had *never* talked about that, but just because Emma was so close to him.

'Oh, okay then.'

I didn't know what made it come to me, right then, that picture. Maybe it was that I felt exactly like I had the day I found him. Crazy. Only now it was a fucking test, and that day it had been ...

I'd kept it out of my head since ... Did I even *ever* remember it? It was weird. Now that it was here of course I remembered, but it was like those photos Tracey had given me. Once I made myself stop remembering, I was pretty good at keeping it up. But now that it was back, I couldn't make it go away again.

The week before Christmas. Nearly a year ago. It had been my job to check on him by that time, not just a pleading suggestion from Mom. My job, because Dad was at work and Mom had to be there for Emma, who *wasn't* in the hospital for once, but was only going to school for half of the day because that is as long as she could make it before she was exhausted.

Plus, I guess it just made sense, because I was in town for school, and I could just walk up the hill during my lunch hour.

He wasn't well. We all knew he was going to die. But no one expected that he was going to die *that day*. Mom was spending most nights talking to him on the phone, trying to get him to at least consider the hospice. They had a place for him.

She tried to tell him it was nice place. It wasn't like a hospital, because there was nothing they could do for him in an actual hospital. It was too late for their toxic drugs. There was nothing they could give him, and if he wasn't a customer for the drug companies, then he didn't belong there. Not that he would have gone anyway.

He wouldn't leave his house. To be honest, I couldn't blame him. Why go live in a stinking house filled with other dying people when you could fade away in your own house, brimming with dignity? He had that in spades as long as he was in his house.

So we had to go there to take care of him, without him actually knowing that we were taking care of him. *I* had to go to him most of the time.

I did tell you just how much he liked me, didn't I? He

tolerated me. Barely. I had too many opinions. I was 'surly'. I showed no 'promise'. I was not a proper child like my sister was. As if he knew what a proper child was. How could he know? He hadn't even raised his own daughter.

But despite the fact that he almost always greeted me with, 'Humph. You again.' I didn't mind going. I could tolerate Grandad too. Because I loved his house.

I don't think that people under say, probably Grandad's age, are supposed to truly love houses. It isn't a conversation I have ever had with my friends. They might like the idea of their future bungalows, with all the latest, greatest in decorating, but that doesn't mean that they do, or will, *love* a house. Same with my parents. My mom spent months picking out everything she needed to have before she would move into our fixer-upper when I was twelve. Finally, she was going to live in a house they owned.

She didn't love it though. It had been a stepping stone. She had been so sure that once she had her qualifications and started to build her practice, it was only a matter of time before we would be moving onto some quaint hobby farm, complete with a workshop for dad, which he would need after he quit his job at the mine and started to do art again.

Houses to most people seem to be tied up with all sorts of other things that are not the houses themselves.

But I *loved* Grandad's house. From the time I was tiny it had seemed like some kind of magical place. There was his office of course, full of books and everything serious, with an honest to goodness fireplace. I only went in there when he wasn't though. Too intimidating otherwise. With him behind that massive desk. It was only my room when he wasn't in it.

And the round room, which you had to climb all of these stairs to get to. Once you were up there though, you had this 360-degree view of Kendal all below you. You could play that you were Rapunzel in the tower room. Or that you were the king and that everyone below you was part of your kingdom.

But I loved more than anything in the world the little attic room, with the window seat, even though it only looked out into the trees behind the house. I loved sitting there and doing absolutely nothing. Just sitting and soaking up all of the safe comfort of that house.

It is hard to put into words what I felt for that place. Maybe all of the love that I wanted to feel for Grandad went into my feelings for his house instead.

But that day.

I could only do it again – go in that door again through memory – because I could feel the sure, sure of Farley's heart under my ear.

I thought that Granddad wasn't there. He had given me a key to put under the flower pot, so that I could let myself in. I wasn't even sure that he could have made it down the stairs from his bedroom at that point if he wanted to. But this way, he could acknowledge as little as possible the fact that his daughter was sending me to check on him. All he had to do was pretend that he was asleep. And I knew that is what he did most of the time.

That is why I thought he was out that day. Usually, when I came in the door I would hear him shuffling to the bed. He'd hear the key in the lock, but somehow it never occurred to him that if he could hear me coming in, then obviously I could hear him. PhD be damned, he wasn't that smart sometimes.

But that day – nothing.

He could have been *actually* sleeping. Somehow I never thought of that at all. I didn't hear him and I assumed he wasn't there.

So I was happy. I had already cancelled the last two classes in my mind. Straight up to the attic room, that is where I was headed. And no geriatric duty. That is honestly what I was thinking. I was such a cow.

But what he did to me was worse.

I got to the first landing, with no sound from his bedroom. None. Even though I just knew that he wasn't there, I thought I better peek in the door to make sure that he wasn't.

Thinking about it now, it didn't make sense. Where the fuck did I think he had gone? Popped out for a bit of shopping? He had home help every morning and evening to feed him, to give him his pain medication, to wipe his ass. What the hell made me think he had just stepped out the door for a few errands? Somehow, the house felt empty.

Well I guess it was.

When I opened the door to his bedroom — without knocking — because I was so sure he wasn't there — there he was. Sort of. Bits of him were. Everywhere. Red everywhere. Red where there shouldn't have been red.

I closed my eyes tighter, pushing the image with all of my might away. Bringing every photo, every drawing I had done in the last week in front of it. Covering it. I wouldn't let it be true. I'd made it up. Just like thinking the test today had been the wrong test. I had been wrong about that, I could be wrong about this too.

I tried to tell myself the story I had re-written for that day, making it the story I could bear, with all the blood carefully covered up: *I hadn't checked on him at all that day. Sometimes I didn't. Sometimes I didn't check and I just said I did. When Mom asked had I checked on him, I'd told her I hadn't, that I'd had no time. She had believed me, and that's the truth we had all embraced.* If you retell yourself a story enough times, you make it true. That's what happened.

It had been Mom who found him. She'd come home and told us. The cancer had beaten him. That is what she told us. That was what I remembered. That was what I remembered. That was what I remembered.

Farley's shirt was wet under my head. My ear was filling up with liquid. It made my heart stop for a moment, and then start to beat again faster, but when I put my hand under my head and brought it out again, my hand wasn't red.

There were only tears, no blood.

Farley had to wake me up when we got to Red River. I'd fallen asleep to the rhythm of his heart. But I felt better. Still fuzzy, but better. The pictures had stopped.

'Do you want to go somewhere and talk about it?' Farley asked. It was the last thing I wanted to do.

The terrible video in my head was covered tightly now and I wanted to keep it that way. I'd been doing too much drawing and not sleeping much at all. I couldn't remember when I had slept more than three hours in a night. It was wrecking my head, making all sorts of wild pictures come into my head. That was just one of them.

I'd make it go away. I *remembered* Mom coming home and telling us Grandad had died. I *remembered* that I wasn't home that day and she rang me and rang me on her way home, until I finally answered. She had wanted to make sure I was there when she arrived, that she had something to tell us.

I didn't want to talk about it with Farley, I wanted it to

stay away.

'You have to teach a lesson,' I said instead.

'But ...'

'No, really.' I willed my head to clear, to put on a proper expression, because I couldn't seem to tell what my face was doing. He still sat there, and the driver was standing at the front of the aisle, waiting for us to get off. 'I haven't been to see Emma in ages. I've got to go see her. I'm okay. It's just ... I'm okay.' It was almost true.

'Jane, we are so far out of polite conversation territory that you can't possibly think I believe that.'

'Ok,' I tried again, because I *needed* him to go. 'I don't know if I'm okay. But if we get off this bus, and I go to see if my sister is okay, then I might be okay.'

He nodded and gave me the briefest squeeze before he got up. He didn't say a word, just got off the bus. Only when he was gone did I appreciate that I had just sent away the one bit of my life I was certain about. I could count my lucky star for sending him my way. Thinking that, made me glad that Farley couldn't actually read my mind; he would have never let me live that thought down.

I forgot that I hate going to the hospital in the morning,

when everything is at its most hospital-ness. That's when the nurses change bedding, and there are piles of piss-smelling sheets in bins everywhere. That's when groups of interns trail after doctors with their clipboards, looking important and scared all at the same time. And I didn't need to see scared; I'd had enough of that. I didn't need to see important either. Important hadn't done a thing to help Emma.

Maybe I need to outline Emma's medical history here. I really haven't wanted to. This isn't actually Emma's story, it's mine, but I guess it might be important to know what has kept me in limbo for three years.

It's a pretty average story I would guess, despite not feeling very average to my family of course. At first, the doctors all thought that Emma had hurt her knee. You would kind of expect that since she was going to dance lessons three times a week and twirling around the house every other day. It can't be good for you all that exercise. So the doctors just sent her to physiotherapy. And Mom had to ferry her around to those appointments on top of the dancing.

But I guess it was just getting worse. Apparently she was waking up in the night with pain. Truly, I don't remember any of this. I wasn't paying attention. It was just my little sister being kind-of whiney in that way that only makes her seem sweeter because she only does it in a quiet way. At the time, I was thinking more about my own life – and I've told you how that was going. I wasn't exactly joining sports teams and putting my name forward for student council. That time is all a bit of a blur to be honest.

So eventually she got the cancer diagnosis, a tumour on her knee. That was fine. Well it wasn't fine, but it didn't feel too bad at first, as cancer goes. Maybe it was just because I got the watered down version of how things were going to go. Looking back, I'm sure it wasn't fine for Mom and Dad. What I got told though, was that Emma was going to be in the hospital for a short stay while she got some chemotherapy, then she was going to have surgery where they would take out the tiny, tiny tumour, and then a bit more chemotherapy to make sure every cancer cell was gone. It was going to be a bit of a pity, because Emma wouldn't be able to dance for nearly a year, but all would be fine.

I only found out slowly that even in the best scenario that process was probably going to be more than a year. There wasn't any talk of days in hospital turning into weeks either, when there were complications with infection and only Mom was allowed in the room with Emma. Or of the possibility that the cancer would spread to her lungs, requiring more surgery and stronger drugs.

I think if doctors told you that stuff, whole families might just decide to drink a jug of poison-laced Kool-aid. The good thing about cancer seems to be that the bad news only comes in drips, so it doesn't seem too terrible. Maybe all tragic things are like that. Sometimes I wonder if war might be like that. Like if tanks started rolling down our street, I would think, 'Well, they're kind of like cars, only bigger. Not that big of a deal.' And then when people were being shot the next town over, 'Well, I didn't know them that well.' And then, 'Well, at least it wasn't us,' when the enemy started shooting our neighbours. Maybe by the time you start losing your family members, you are too numb to even comprehend that this is really bad.

And then, just like in war, life has to keep happening. Nobody ever said to me, just take a few months off school. Nobody said that to Dad about his job either. We just have to keep doing it day after fucking day. Doctors don't talk about that at all. We're like the civilian casualties of war that nobody wants to talk about. We don't exist.

That is kind of what I was thinking about as I forgot to waste time, and walked toward the hospital instead. I was actually having a bit of a private rant about it as I walked in the sliding glass doors of the lobby. I don't know why I decided to get angry about it all then. Maybe I needed something to focus on, something to keep my mind in one direction, because it didn't want to do that. I needed to focus on something that wasn't my fault like the test had been, something that made sense, something I knew. Emma's illness was something I knew.

It was definitely not the right day to go into the hospital early. Rounds were in full swing, and worse, the swarm was surrounding Emma's bed. No one even noticed me come into the room. They were all leaning in to hear the whole story. Mom's back was to me, but I could see that both her hands were holding one of Em's, which was the most she could do to shield her from having to hear her history for probably the thousandth time. You'd think they could issue her with earmuffs, or better yet, just write the story out, and photocopy it. The interns could have an interesting book, collecting all these medical stories by the end of their term. I'm sure they'd like that sort of thing.

'... resistant osteosarcoma. While the standard treatment of surgical removal, followed by doxorubin and cisplatin has eradicated the remaining tumour in the left lung, and the left lateral meniscus remains tumour free, we now have the significant complication of the patient's tertiary sarcoma site.'

'The patient' did not seem to be even listening.

'Current chemotherapy treatment has been ceased, as the patient was not tolerating side effects, and the patient assessed for her suitability for the clinical trial of Everolimus. In the meantime, IMRT is to be commenced tomorrow morning, and options for limb salvage discussed.'

I'd slid down to sit against the wall by the door, to stay out of the way, and I had almost been tuning out. But some of the words in the story were new. 'Limb salvage'? What were they talking about?

'Haven't studies shown that Everolimus treatment with young women had a significant chance of impacting fertility? Have all other options been explored?' That was Dr Jonathan. I liked that he was questioning the suggested poison, but I was more concerned about the casual way limb salvage had been thrown out. I thought we'd gotten past that talk at least. Every test in the past two years had shown Emma's leg to be cancer free. It had been the saving grace. Okay, it wasn't so great that bits of cancer kept showing up in her lungs, but the doctors kept insisting that there was lots of lung material to spare.

'This is a particularly aggressive tumour, Dr Ballerini,' the grey-haired doctor, who I kind of recognised, said. 'It is a sizable tumour in the femur. I believe possible side effects are the least of our worries.'

I waited for Mom to say something. Wasn't this a bit of a shock? It was the first I had heard of it. Why was she sitting there, still holding Emma's hand like he was talking about the weather?

'Prognosis?' Dr Jonathan persisted, turning a little red though. 'For the leg I mean.' He looked over at Emma then.

Dr Grey Hair waited a second before he answered, peering over the top of his glasses at his intern. I don't think he was waiting so that he came up with the right words to spare Emma hurt. I think it was a power thing; he couldn't let Dr Jonathan get the upper hand.

'Dr Ballerini, we are in the business of saving lives. The prognosis of limbs is secondary. I am afraid we have given too much consideration to complete salvage already.' He hung Emma's clipboard up at that, moving toward the door without even saying anything to Emma.

I had to stand up because if I didn't I would be on the floor, in the middle of the swarm, as they moved toward the door, but also because I could not believe what I had just heard. And this is a thing I do sometimes. I can't seem to help it. I don't keep my inflammatory statements in my head. Not even for a few minutes to think about whether I should – which quite frankly is almost all of the time.

'Dr Whitman.' I had remembered his name. He'd never actually ever spoken directly to me, but I'd been in the room a few times in the early days, when he explained all the cancereze terms to my parents. 'You cannot be serious! My sister's leg is not 'secondary'. Both of them are pretty much primary to who she is!'

I was kind of aware that my voice was louder than it needed to be, but it just seemed to want to come out that loudly. Dr Whitman was used to emotional outbursts though, and he had his tactics. He moved toward me and put his hand on my shoulder. Patted my shoulder in fact. And then he moved toward the door before I could say another word.

'Jane!' My mother wasn't so skilled in how to handle emotional outbursts. She had let go of Emma's hand now, but she looked ashen, like she was the one who needed someone to hold her hand.

'Mom, you knew about this!' I hurled. 'You think it's okay? You think that it's okay to go through three years of this bullshit, only to have the very thing Emma doesn't want thrown in her face like there isn't a choice!'

'Jane Ellen!' Her voice was almost a whisper, but her tone was acidic. I couldn't remember when she had last used my middle name; it had been ages since she had gotten angry at me. 'This is NOT the place, nor is it the time.'

'Oh yeah?' I was on a roll now. 'And when was the time you were going to tell me? I suppose you were going to tell me when she was out of surgery, like you did after her knee surgery? It's fantastic the way you include me. I'm sure you must get so many compliments on your parenting skills.' There was a weird buzzing in my head when I stopped talking. Mom just looked at me with utter contempt, and Emma didn't look at me at all. I tried to take a breath, to stop the buzzing, but the silence was worse. Pictures started flashing in my head again – x-rays, bottles of drugs, a severed leg on a stainless steel table – Emma's leg, with her pink princess slipper still on the foot. I shut my eyes to try to make the pictures go away.

'Jane!' Mom's voice sounded far away.

'You just take it, Mom,' I was talking again before I could stop myself, talking fast now, before she could shut me down. 'You let them pump her full of poison. Methotrexate, Topotecin, Doxorubicin, Ifosfamide, Etoposide.' I rattled off all the drug names that Emma had been given, names I didn't even think I had known. They came flying into my head now.

'I wonder how much those drugs cost. I wonder who is profiting. I'm sure someone is. While people collect their little piles of coins for Emma in the shops to make themselves feel better, some big drug companies are collecting their millions from hospitals like this one that keep pumping the poison into kids' arms, even when there is hardly any arm left to pump it into.' The words just kept spilling out. The more I talked the more the words came.

'You heard Dr Ballerini. The drugs are poison—but the doctors won't listen because they're probably being paid by the drug companies too. You've got to wonder if there was ever anything wrong with Emma in the first place.'

'Stop it, Jane. Nobody said anything like that. You are not making sense.' Mom's voice was shrill and panicked, but I couldn't stop.

'And now, after there's no more money to be made from the drugs, they're just going to cut off Emma's leg and throw it away. Or maybe we get to take it home to hang a lamp shade on. I can't let that happen. You know it can't happen.'

The sound of Emma crying made me stop. I could see her, but she was like this picture that I couldn't get to, couldn't feel. She seemed like a moving picture of herself. The buzzing in my head was getting louder and it felt like the walls were moving in on us. I tried to breathe, but I couldn't seem to get any air into my lungs. I had to get out.

When I walked into the hall, it wasn't better. The pictures kept running through my head – piles of pills, piles of legs, white coated doctors moving toward Emma with saws. I walked down hallways, willing my mind to stop. Stop, stop, stop. I kept walking – right, left, left, left, right. I kept walking. I didn't know where I was. I'd been in this hospital hundreds of times, and I didn't know where I was. And I couldn't breathe.

There was a line of chairs against a wall, with no one sitting in them so I sat down and put my head between my knees. Was that what you were supposed to do for shock? That was what this was – shock. I just had to calm down.

My head was still upside down when I felt a hand on my shoulder. The picture of Dr Whitman so patronisingly patting my shoulder rose, and I bolted upright. I wanted to slap him.

It wasn't him though; it was Dr Jonathan.

'Mind if I sit down?' For a moment I was confused, feeling like I was back on the bus, with Farley asking the same question, but the blue coat brought me back. I think I must have nodded, because he did sit. My head was still buzzing, but I was feeling a little calmer. Not calm enough to open my mouth though. There were still words piling up in my throat that would spill out if I did. I kept it shut.

'That was pretty brave, standing up to Dr Whitman like that,' he said.

I still couldn't open my mouth. I was afraid of what might come out. It didn't stop the words from looping back up through my brain though. Methotrexate, Topotecin, Doxorubicin, Ifosfamide, Etoposide, limb salvage, osteosarcoma, resistant osteosarcoma, aggressive sarcoma. The pictures kept up the slide show too, flashing fast and furious, with words and dates underneath. *Osteosarcoma tumour November 2012, Surgery one December 2012, Methotrexate January to February 2013* … A slideshow documenting Emma's history going through my mind.

'You are right to question Emma's treatment.' He was smiling at me like some kind of Jesus. 'It isn't the only way.'

The pictures stopped. The buzzing stopped. The words stopped. Utter relief poured in.

I looked at Dr Jonathan and he had this weird glow around him. Okay, he didn't. It was just the light behind him, coming in the window, but I swear what he said was the clearest thing I have ever heard in my life. *It isn't the only way.*

I couldn't talk. I wanted to hear every word he said.

'I can't talk about it here, obviously.' He turned, and looked over his shoulder, and then he stood up quickly. 'But listen carefully. You'll hear the truth, if you listen carefully.' He flashed me that Jesus smile before he continued down the hall as if he had not just uttered the most important words I would ever hear.

I'm not sure how many halls I wandered before I found the glass doors leading to freedom. It didn't matter anymore. There was another way! Emma was going to get better and she most certainly was not going to lose her leg. For the first time in three years there was hope of escaping this death trap we were caught in. I had been too mired down, just going through the motions. I hadn't been able to think clearly enough to even question what was happening in this awful institution. Mom and Dad obviously were not going to see it. They believed everything they were told. How long had Dr Jonathan been trying to tell me there was another way?

It didn't matter now. He'd found a way to tell me and I was going to find out the truth.

It took me a moment to remember that it was Saturday when I woke up. It was getting more difficult to keep the days straight without enough classes to give me anchor points.

The night before I hadn't gone over to Dell's either. Every night I had sworn that tonight was the night. Last night I had forgotten to even do that. Two Friday nights without him now. Weird.

I always go to Dell's on Friday nights. Usually he buys us pizza, and sometimes we go over to his friend Dave's house – especially since Dave has started going out with Kelly-the-hairdresser. It is all properly grown up. I feel like I am twelve on those nights, but I would rather feel twelve and out of place, than to feel like this was my life, like Brenda does. Or maybe that's not true. Maybe I tell myself that because part of me wishes that I could be happy with this life, like Brenda is happy with hers.

Anyway, I hadn't gone to Dell's, so I didn't know whether I had missed a double date or not. I walked into the bath-room with my phone, trying to remember if Dell had texted me the night before, if I had actually replied with an excuse for not coming over like I'd been meaning to do all week. I seemed to have turned it off. Nine missed calls and five text messages lit up the screen when it came back to life, answering my question.

For a moment I felt bad about all of those unanswered calls and messages, and then I remembered that I had turned the phone off *because* the phone had not stopped beeping at me. It had seemed really important not to be interrupted. Not that I had been any place where it would have been a problem to be interrupted. I'd come home, taken out note pads, and started writing down every single thing that I remembered between when Emma had been diagnosed and now. There was a lot to remember. The phone beeping at me had become irritating. But then the house phone had rang as well, so after I took the call from Dad, who said he was going to the hospital when his shift ended, I took that phone off the hook too.

Three years was a lot of stuff to try to remember, and I didn't need any interruptions. But even with none, and even though I made notes, and then drawings – the drawings seemed to jog more memories than words – until after 5am, I didn't seem to be any closer to understanding what Dr Jonathan had been trying to tell me.

I looked at my phone again, this time to figure out if I should eat breakfast or lunch. It had to be late. There were no sounds of Dad, so he must have already left again.

The time. I forgot that I wanted to know the time. I felt all disoriented with staying up until nearly dawn, and sleeping late. Why wasn't Mom here yet?

I switched the phone on again. 8:04. For a moment I thought that maybe I had slept the whole day through, but it was too light for that. It really was only eight in the morning. I couldn't seem to sleep anymore.

I had a brainwave. Another reason to be up at such an ungodly hour. I would start the cleaning. I could maybe even finish most of it before Mom got home.

I needed to *do* something, and for once, it didn't feel like an impossible task. It actually felt fantastic. Three cups of coffee had me buzzing – in a good way, not the fuzzy, scary buzz of the day before, but pure caffeine induced energy. I put the radio on and leapt about the place like I was Annie *and* all of her orphan side-kicks.

The kitchen, with the week's dishes on the verge of falling off every counter, was suddenly a challenge I could tackle. I didn't stop with the dishes. I cleaned the fridge, and the oven, and every cupboard. I got down on my knees and scrubbed every inch of the floor. Literally, with a scrubbing brush I found way behind the drain pipe under the sink.

I don't think I have ever looked at the room the same way by the time I was through with it. It was pure pride. I felt like taking photos and posting them on every site, though a tiny part of me did realise that would be a bit weird, so I didn't.

Instead, I moved onto other rooms. The more I cleaned, the more I saw that needed cleaning. I forgot that I was going to eat breakfast – yes, it was definitely breakfast I was going to eat. I couldn't remember eating any dinner the night before, so I must be starving. I thought I must be. But I kept going because I wanted to get the house spotless before Mom got home. She would probably be bringing us something to eat anyway.

I remembered how angry she had been with me the day before. I'd never seen that look of loathing before. If Dr Jonathan hadn't have found me, talked to me, I would probably still have been wallowing in that look, inventing ever more cutting retorts to that look, ready to hurl at Mom the moment she walked in.

That seemed a little ridiculous now though. She was just tired. We had all been tired. How could we not be, slogging through week after week, month after month, of the same old thing? I'd felt the same way until Dr Jonathan confirmed that I was right – that we didn't have to accept every damn thing that the hospital threw at us.

I wanted Mom to come home and smile, to feel like she could sit down, and we could have lunch together. I was going to give her that. I could make her happy. We could forget about the day before.

That was my line of thought while I did more cleaning in four hours than I had probably done in my entire life. I am not exaggerating. I suddenly understood Mom's exasperation at how little I ever achieved in the cleaning department. It wasn't that hard. It really wasn't. How had I missed that?

I actually ran out of things to clean. At least, I ran out of things to clean that had ever occurred to me to clean. As I lay on the sofa, looking at the ceiling and feeling completely smug with myself, I did begin to wonder if ceilings get cleaned. Did they need to be cleaned? Dirt would settle on surfaces, and with gravity, you would think that ceilings would just stay white, but did they? I started to go through all of the possibilities. Smoke. It would rise. But nobody in our house smoked. We didn't even have a fireplace; we had a gas thing that looked like a fire burning instead. Dad had fought for a real one. We had a chimney. But Mom didn't want a fireplace – because of the smoke. That would get on the ceiling and need to be cleaned. I was safe. I could skip the ceiling.

Where was she anyway? I had lost track of time again. That sense of the time of day was evading me.

When I found my phone again there were three more missed calls. None were from Mom though. Or Dad. I was going to have to ring Dell back soon, though first I had to come up with some pretty good excuse as to why I hadn't called before now, not kept my promise of staying away for only a week. For some reason I couldn't seem to attach the guilt I should feel to that thought. Now that I had finished rushing around the house, I had a sudden urge to go back to my notes.

I found Mom's number and rang her instead.

'Jane!' Mom answered straight away.

'Hi, Mom.' It felt strange to talk. I hadn't uttered a single word to anyone for nearly twenty-four hours, even though my head had been spitting out thoughts with hardly a break.

'I'm sorry, hon. I was meant to be home hours ago.' The anger of yesterday seemed to have left her. Me too.

'Were you? What time is it?' I asked, surprised that she was that late.

'Dad's here still, and we're coming home soon. Both of us,' she said. I hadn't heard that decisiveness in here voice for months. It made me a bit nostalgic — that was the Mom I knew, even though it had more often than not been directed at what I should be doing, but wasn't.

'So … will I wait here for you?' I wasn't sure what I was supposed to say to that, because it didn't fit our pattern.

Mom and Dad and me, together on a Saturday afternoon, without Emma, was not what we did. I had a sinking feeling that it was a bad conversation she planned to have. She didn't know one thing that I was starting to figure out, so of course she was just going to accept anything the hospital told her. She was completely in their web. I was certain that Dad was as well.

'Sweetie, we need to have a chat with you. It hasn't been an easy day here.'

That's when I knew that I definitely could not be here when they got back. I felt like I was going to choke. I couldn't breathe again. My stomach started to heave and I put the phone down, and ran to the toilet. I didn't know how I had anything in my stomach to throw up.

Was it Grandad? But I already knew. I already knew, and she didn't know I knew. I didn't want to be here to hear it again. But of course it wasn't Grandad. That was ages ago.

I tried to calm down, to stop that memory. Because it *was* a memory. I'd always known it was; I just didn't want it there in my head.

And it was time to see Dell.

'I'm coming over,' I said as soon as he answered. There wasn't any point in going into everything with him over the phone. He'd answered, so I knew he'd forgive me for not getting back to him before now. Dell didn't have it in him to get mad anyway. That's why we were so good together.

It wasn't until I was on my way over to his house that it occurred to me that I maybe should have at least changed my clothes. I was still wearing the jeans and hoodie that I had been wearing the day before, and now I had cleaned an entire house in them. I wasn't concerned enough to turn around and go back to change though.

The window was closed and still locked when I got there and I knocked to let Dell know I was here. I guessed that he hadn't opened it since I had been here last. Two weeks without it being used as my front door. I hadn't put on a jacket when I left my house, and the closed window reminded me that I was pretty cold. For a second, the fact that I didn't have a jacket on kind of panicked me – not because I thought I was in danger of freezing to death or anything, but because a jacket isn't really something anyone just forgot to put on in Canada in December. It was weird even for me.

My head was so full of everything else, I couldn't keep things straight. Why wasn't my head working?

It was Dr Jonathan's fault; I hadn't been able to think properly since he'd got me thinking of what was happening in the hospital. But what did a little forgetfulness matter when I needed most of my brain to think about what he had told me, to listen to what was going to save Emma's leg. I could see my list of dates and drugs. November 2012 – Methotexate, February to March 2012 – Ifosfamide and Etoposide. The list covered several pages. I'd written everything out, but now I needed to find out more about those drugs. There was probably a connection between them.

Thinking about it made the nightmare hospital slideshow

start up in my head again. And I was suddenly panicked about the pictures that would follow.

I banged on the window again – hard. I had to see Dell before THAT picture came back. If he didn't answer soon I was going to have to go.

It was too cold to be standing around outside.

The window slid open finally and I made a very ungraceful entrance through it, catching my toe on the frame and ending up landing in a half summersault at Dell's feet. I mumbled some sort of apology and stood up.

'Sorry, I was upstairs. I didn't think you'd get here so fast,' Dell said. 'Do you want something to eat? I'm just making some pasta.'

'Sure, okay,' I said, even though the thought of eating made my stomach churn.

Dell headed up the stairs, but I didn't follow him. My legs felt all wobbly and I had to sit down. Sit down and try to think clearly enough to say something to Dell. I didn't know what I was going to say though.

It felt weird being in Dell's house, like I had never been there before. I'd never noticed how dingy it was. The ceiling was so low that I always felt like my head would hit it, even though I wasn't tall enough to worry about that. Everything was brown. Dark wood panelled walls, geometric brown patterns marching across the carpet, swirling brown flowers on the sagging sofa. Everything sepia coloured, like the room had been photo shopped.

And the smell. There was that damp, musty smell that basements always seem to have, but with overlays of unwashed dishes and dirty socks. I was feeling sick again.

This had been my comfortable spot. My hideaway. It didn't feel like that anymore. Now it felt claustrophobic. Stale air that was depleted of oxygen. Thinking of that made me feel like I wasn't getting enough, like I might pass out from breathing air with no oxygen. I got up and opened the window that Dell had shut.

I had a sudden urge to climb back through it. I couldn't do this, couldn't be here again. But Dell was coming down the stairs, balancing two plates, so I sat back down. He glanced at the open window, the blinds clattering against it with each gust of wind, but he didn't say anything.

He didn't say anything at all. Just sat down and started to eat. It was the kind of pasta you made from a package. Shrivelled brown specks that were supposed to be mushrooms floating in the watery sauce. I couldn't eat it. I watched Dell's plate instead. He was silent as he ate, his fork hitting the plate each time he shovelled up a bite sounding like a bell ringing out. There wasn't even the soundtrack of a game to drown it out.

'I don't know what to say, Dell.'

Finally, he put his fork down, and I still couldn't look at him. Not his face.

'Are you staying? Are you back?'

When I raised my eyes to his face I couldn't stop the memory from flooding back, exploding in full colour.

'Dell, you came and got me!' THAT memory was starting, like I'd just pressed play and couldn't reach the stop button.

'What?' He looked at me quizzically. 'What are you talking about?'

'You know what I'm talking about.' It was all flooding back. All of it.

I had stood there, frozen. It was like liquid nitrogen had been poured over me, making it impossible for any bit of me to move. Except my eyes. And what I saw hadn't made sense, not in a way you can think about. It was like the awful, horrendous scene in front of me could not be real. I didn't want it to be real. But I couldn't stop seeing it. Couldn't stop seeing it, but couldn't make it real, tangible, something that actually existed.

It seemed ages before I began to thaw. My phone had been in my pocket, and that's when I rang Dell. Feet still frozen, the splattered blood nearly reaching them, Grandad's body, and half his head in front of me, I pulled out my phone and rang Dell.

'Can you come and get me in Kendal?' I'd asked.

'I'm at work.'

'I know. But I really need you to come get me right now.' My voice had been so steady, so sure, that it felt like it wasn't my own.

'I'm off in an hour. Can you wait until then? What's so important?'

'Trust me, it's pretty important, Dell. I really need you to pick me up right now.'

And he had. By the time he had come for me, I had been standing on the front porch, key put under the flower pot where it was always kept. But that was as far as I could get. I'd stood there for nearly an hour, not even able to go back into the entrance way where it was warmer. That image of Grandad's room had refused to get out of my head.

Dell had saved me. Seeing him had made it go away. He had let me walk away. Let me pretend that I had never found what I did. He didn't ask questions; he didn't want to know. He let me leave and let the home care lady, who would be in at five, find him instead.

Only, she wasn't the one who came. She called in sick, and there was nobody to cover. Mom went instead. I made Mom have to live with that image. I made Mom, who had only had her dad for a small part of her life, have the last image of him be *that*.

And Dell had let me. Even when I tried to tell him what

I'd found, and couldn't, he had let me not tell him. Finally, when I couldn't get any other words out I just said he was dead – nothing more. And then I had begged him to not say that I had been there, that I couldn't be the one tell my mom about it, and he had let me just leave.

I don't know how long I sat there, remembering this. Maybe not long, but I knew what to say now.

'Dell, I was never here in the first place. Not really.' I tried to say it kindly, even though I'm not really good at that sort of thing. It was the truth. I had sat here, in this room, several evenings a week for almost a year since then, but I hadn't been here at all. Because how could that have been me? How could it, if I'd spent all of those nights without a single word, without a single *thought* about that day?

I wanted it to end that way. It felt as true, and right as it could be. But of course, I was only one half of this break up. This being my first one, I didn't have a lot of experience with them, but I'd heard enough to know that they were

221

not always pretty.

'What's *wrong* with you, Jane?' That was enough to make it impossible for me to contain everything that wanted to spill out.

'What is wrong with me? How can you ask that?' I could barely hear myself above the buzzing in my head. It was there as suddenly as if someone had turned a volume control on an amp too far. 'How could you let me forget? How could you not ask me one single thing about that day? Didn't you wonder what was wrong? This room is like a black hole, sucking everything from me. Who knows what I'll forget next. I could have almost forgotten Emma, sitting here talking about nothing, doing nothing. Rotting. Rotting. Rotting.' The words brought pictures of rotting flesh flashing, flashing through my brain.

'Stop shouting,' Dell's voice sounded more like a whisper. 'My dad is sleeping. Let me——'

I wanted to let him finish, I wanted to shut up; I just couldn't. The words at the back of my brain were pushing and shoving to get out.

'I'll tell you what's wrong. Everything is wrong, really wrong, because I shouldn't be here while Emma is in that torture chamber. How is she there when it should be me? Because I would have figured it out, if it was me. I'd know that something is fucking wrong when you have your body pumped with drug after drug for three years and yet you are still getting worse and worse. I would have known there was something wrong with that. I would have looked into it, would have figured out the drug companies were controlling the hospital, the doctors, all of it. But instead, here I am, doing nothing. And you are letting me.'

'Please, Jane, stop.' I knew I was out of control. I knew he was right, but I couldn't stop.

'I can't do this anymore ...' Seeing Dell's dad at the top of the stairs, looking like he wanted to kill someone, did stop me. There wasn't much guess work in figuring out who he wanted to kill.

'You bloody well WON'T do this anymore!' he boomed. He came charging down the stairs.

'Dad, hold on,' Dell pleaded.

For a moment I thought he really might kill me, when he grabbed my arm. I would have deserved it. Waking someone working night shift at the mine was about the worst thing you could do.

It turned out he wasn't going to kill me, but he wasn't going to put up with any more noise either. He started to march me, bouncer-style, up the stairs.

'Dad, I really think there's something wrong with Jane,' Dell shouted up the stairs, as Alan opened the door and shoved me out of it, with not a word. It wasn't until the door slammed behind me that I understood what Dell had been trying to say.

I stood on the doorstep, trying to slow my thoughts to process the last fifteen minutes. I wanted to feel relief at having ended it, but all I felt was dread, and fear. The horrible, hurtful words wouldn't stop hurling through my brain. For once I was glad that Alan was such an ass. He'd saved me from attacking his son any more than I already had. *What is wrong with you, Jane?* That was a question I just couldn't think about.

I went to the park instead of going home. I couldn't go home. I felt too jumpy for that.

The night before, sitting with my drawings and notes, I had felt focused and sure. Now everything felt wrong and upside down and I couldn't stop the pictures in my head. I felt like crying it was hurting so much trying to keep them out.

I sat down on one of the swings and tried to put my sweatshirt over my hands so I could hold the chains without touching the freezing metal. As soon as I started to pump my legs, pulling hard on the chains to reach the highest point I could, I started to feel like I could breathe again. I was a kid who had spent hours on swings and I still secretly loved them. I'd never grown out of that feeling you get in the pit of your stomach when you drop down, falling, with only a bit of old tyre under you to ensure you don't hit the ground.

The pictures faded. The buzzing quieted. I closed my eyes and let myself get lost in the pendulum.

I'd meant to waste an hour or so, and get in the door just about the time my parents were falling asleep in front of the television. I was pretty certain that's where they would be.

Somehow though, it was now 11:30pm and all of the lights were off in the house. Something was happening to the time. I was so used to there being too much of it, and now suddenly it was disappearing.

The door was locked and I had to find the key under the mat to let myself in. Mom didn't know that Dad and I never locked the door when she stayed at the hospital. All of the things that she was usually in charge of just didn't happen at all when she wasn't here. It had begun to feel weirdly like I was a guest the nights that she actually was home, like the dishevelled mess Dad and I usually lived in transformed itself into a Bed and Breakfast, with its list of rules to be followed.

I wanted to sleep, to fall into nothingness. I got into bed and tried to do that. But there were too many images when I closed my eyes. Too many words still running through my brain. About Grandad. About Emma. About Dell. Nothing would stop.

So I turned on the light again. There were so many papers all over the floor. Mine had been the only room I hadn't cleaned. I was certain there were patterns there; and I hadn't wanted to move the papers in case I covered up the links. It had felt like I was close to finding what Dr Jonathan was trying to tell me I should find. I just needed to put the pieces together, to find an alternative to what the hospital was saying was going to happen. I knew what was coming. Of course I did.

I tried to pick up my notes, to make sense of them, but my hands weren't working so well. There seemed to be red blotches all over them. Jesus, of course they weren't working well, I had been outside for hours.

I hadn't had gloves, or a jacket. How many hours had I been outside? I wanted to worry about this. What was I thinking? And how hadn't I noticed that it was cold; that my hands were losing all feeling? People lose fingers to the cold. These thoughts went through my head, but it was like they couldn't stick long enough for me to really process them.

I just needed to focus. The pictures would stop when I got back to the research I had to do. It was up to me to find out what the hospital was hiding. Now that I had dealt with the Dell situation I should be able to do that. There wouldn't be any more messages and phones ringing to interrupt me.

Sleep was just going to have to wait.

I was up early, but Dad was up earlier. He didn't follow the routine that Mom and I did. I hate morning people, even when they happen to include Dad.

'I was just going to wake you.' He was making pancakes. I looked at the time on the microwave to make sure I wasn't confused again. Nope, it really was only 7:30am, far too early for food.

'What's the rush? It's Sunday.' I poured myself a cup of coffee and stuck my nose over it, trying to block the sickly sweet smell of the pancakes.

'We're going early. Emma wants to talk to us all, to you mostly.'

'What is there to talk to me about? It isn't like I am going to have a say, is there? It isn't like Emma even has a say, not that she would ever go against what the almighty doctors tell her she has to do.' I didn't want to have this conversation — with Dad or with Emma. It was pointless, because it was just going to lead to talking about something that wasn't going to happen. I wouldn't let it happen. I just had to figure out exactly how I would stop it.

'I know this isn't easy for you, Jane. Mom and I are really

worried about you.' He put a plate with two banana pan-cakes in front of me. The smell was nauseating. I was certainly not going to eat them.

'I can't talk about this. If I do, we are both going to regret it.' I got up to leave the room, but Dad put his hand on my shoulder, stopping me.

'Jane, you are going to the hospital with us and you are listening to your sister.'

I was all nerves on the drive. People use that saying, 'all nerves', but I'm not sure they actually know what it means. Today I could feel those nerves firing. Hundreds and thousands of them.

It wasn't just that I didn't want to hear whatever it was that Emma was going to tell me. I pretty much knew what that was anyway. I was afraid to see Emma because for the last day I hadn't been able to see her as whole. She was this jumble of words and pictures. Words and pictures that were making me excited and scared all at the same time. She was a network of cells that were struggling to free themselves from the poisons that invaded through the portal of a needle. I could see those cells shrinking away from the invaders, but I couldn't see Emma in my head anymore.

Only, now I was pretty sure that if the invaders were stopped the damage could be undone. I had a backpack full of notes that had solutions. I just needed help to make sense of them. Dr Jonathan could do that. I knew he could.

Of course, this wasn't something I could share with Emma until I was certain. Today she needed me to keep lying to her, to comfort her about what they were going to do to her. I needed to be her big sister. And I didn't know if I could do that. Everything in my head was moving so fast.

Dad tried to prepare me as we walked through the lobby of the hospital.

'I know you have opinions on this, Jane. But can you just listen to Emma today? Just this once?' Dad had a way of saying things, like nothing else in the world was as important as what he was asking me to do. It always made me *want* to do what he asked, even when I wanted to do the exact opposite.

'I'll try,' I answered honestly, but the buzzing was coming back. It was this building. I couldn't think straight in it.

'She is so afraid, and we need to be strong for her.'

I couldn't do this yet. I would. But not yet.

'Have you got some coins? I just want to get Emma a Fanta.' I tried to sound as casual as I could. It worked. He fished some money out of his pocket.

'I'll meet you up there, okay?'

The words and the pictures were crashing through my head again. Only this time they were chased by Emma's fear. I needed to hurry. I needed to find Dr Jonathan and make him tell me how we could stop Emma from losing her leg, how we could make her better. She couldn't lose any more.

It took me a long time to find him. I walked down every corridor on every floor. He was nowhere.

Then I took out my jumble of notes and I organised them in chronological order. And then I went through them again with highlighters, until the pattern was clear.

It was the pattern that was reassuring me. I needed reassurance. When I was moving or letting the thoughts go, I could see it – that every treatment Emma had undergone in three years was systematically making her worse. Number of drugs administered: increasing in numbers and complexity of regimes. Continuous days in hospital: increasing. Drug companies supplying said drugs: all traced to not more than three. I had dozens of printouts from websites attesting to the detrimental effects of chemotherapy. I had details of two previous lawsuits brought against the hospital. The highlighter showed me the path through all of this.

But when I stopped, I started to doubt myself. It seemed more confusing. I couldn't remember what Dr Jonathan had said to me. I felt like I was missing a piece. I needed to find him.

So I walked again. I walked faster, in case I was missing him, or he was ahead of me and I couldn't catch up. And I let the thoughts crash and crash around my head until the pattern was crystal clear. Of course I could see the pattern no one else could. No one was brave enough to look for it.

No one but myself and Dr Jonathan. When I spotted his blue coat ahead of me on the very bottom floor—the basement – I couldn't stop myself from running. It was perfect. Nobody would overhear our conversation on the morgue floor.

Time had sped again. Two hours gone. Two hours spent in conspiratorial bliss. Everything was so clear now though. It was unbelievable that nobody else could see it.

There was another option for Emma. It had been there in plain sight, but none of the senior doctors wanted to go against the powerful drug companies. It was up to me to fight them. Fight them for Emma's sake.

'Jane, where on earth have you been?' Her question stopped me from feeding another coin into the drink machine. I hadn't expected Mom to come up behind me like that. I had kind of forgotten where I was supposed to be.

'Just a minute.' I couldn't concentrate on putting the right money in the machine *and* answering her. And I really needed a drink.

'Your sister is beside herself worrying about you. You can't just disappear on her. Not today.'

'Sorry, I just got a little caught up talking with Dr Jonathan.' I thought about telling her what we had been discussing, but it didn't seem like a very good idea – not yet anyway.

'What is he doing here on a Sunday, with time to chat?' she said. 'I thought the only place you'd find a doctor here on a Sunday was the emergency operating theatre.'

Mom was not letting me out of her sight again. She even followed me into the toilets when I asked to make a stop on the way. I couldn't blame her I suppose.

I was ready to be there for Emma now though. I was

armed with ammunition. I could take it. I just needed to get through this day. Monday couldn't come soon enough.

Mom didn't lead me to Emma's room. Instead, Dad and Emma were in the 'family room'. I think it's supposed to make you feel like you are not in a hospital, with comfortable sofas and magazines on the end tables. In a way it reminded me of that councillor's office in school, only not so nice. Plus, there was no way you could ignore the hospital smell.

There was nothing comfortable about this room. It oozed hopelessness. Everyone avoided it. Every family of a kid with cancer knew what its purpose really was. This was where families were told the truly bad news. It was even worse when there were families in it for days, waiting, when there was nothing more to tell. I tried not to notice any of the other kids on the ward most of the time, but when this room was in use, you couldn't help it.

Following Mom in the door, I wanted to pick Emma up and carry her back to her bed. Seeing her there, sitting in a chair, wearing a pair of loose jeans and a soft, blue sweater that I had never seen her wear before seemed wrong. It had been weeks since I had seen her out of bed, or dressed. It's not that I exactly liked that, but I hated this more. She was too sick to have to try this hard not to look sick.

'Jane, sit down.' It was Emma, not Mom, directing me. I realised I was still standing in the doorway. Emma held out her hand, ushering me to sit beside her. I'd expected her to

look tired, or sad, or terrified, but there was wasn't one trace
of any of these on her face.

'You know what I'm going to tell you, don't you?' Her
words sounded too grown up for her young voice. I nodded,
not trusting myself to say anything, even though my head
was reasonably quiet. 'There's a new drug that I am going
to be put on. It's been working really well for lots of people.
There's a chance, if this drug works, that my leg could still be
saved, but the tumour in my thigh is pretty big; worse than
the one in my knee was.'

She'd said it in plain language for me. Mom and Dad
already knew all of this of course. They would have been
given the much longer version, with all of its technicalities.
Somewhere in that spiel would have been the dreaded statistics. It's what everyone wants to know – what are the odds of
their kid living? Emma had prepared her spiel carefully for
me, leaving out that detail especially.

She waited for me to say something. I could hear Mom
sniffle, and when I looked over, even Dad had tears in his
eyes. All of this for me, and I couldn't feel it. I had this urge
to unzip my backpack and dump the contents in the middle
of the floor. I gripped the edge of the sofa and tried to concentrate on breathing instead.

'We've spent a lot of time talking with Dr Whitman, and
even other doctors. They'd wait. They'd try the drug, if that's
what I want. Maybe they could save most of the bone. It's

not what they want though.'

'This is a really promising drug though, Emma,' Mom tried to assure her, but Emma didn't even shift her eyes from me.

'The second choice is to give me a titanium rod instead of a thigh bone, and join me all up again. But I'd still have to learn to walk again, and my cancer isn't like most; there's a pretty good chance of another tumour showing up in my lower leg – even with this chemo, even with the rod. I'm not taking that chance. I'm having the whole leg off.'

'Emma!' Mom looked shell shocked. 'That is not what we discussed. That is not what we told Dr Whitman.'

'That is not what *you* told Dr Whitman, Mom.' Emma reached for my hand and I gave it to her. Her voice was getting quieter. I squeezed her hand in support because it was all I could do right now. I so badly wanted to say that she didn't have to lose it, but it wasn't the time. She went on, louder now. 'I am tired of this. I don't want to take more chances, so that, what, maybe I can dance again? It's highly unlikely, and even if it did happen, it isn't worth it.'

'But it is Emma. There's a good chance ...' Mom let her argument go. 'Don't you want the best chance to dance again?'

'If you'd asked me three years ago, probably. But not now. It's too late now.' Her answer was sure. 'Besides, I never knew how much I hated the pressure until I didn't have to do it anymore. Don't you remember, Mom? I used to throw up before almost every performance.'

I'd never known that. All of those times, sharing the back-seat on the way to her performances, when I had thought she was worried, she had probably been concentrating on not puking. I squeezed her hand harder.

Mom nodded.

'Are you sure, Ems?' Dad asked.

'Dad, I just want to live. That's all.' She was getting tired now. Her face was getting that ashen hue of exhaustion. 'Tomorrow. They'll do it tomorrow, if you say yes. Am I letting you down?'

It was so much worse than I'd thought. There were no good choices. Poison Emma or take her leg. I could feel the pictures, the words, start to swirl in my head.

'It's going to be okay, Emma.' Mom was crying, just like she had cried when she came home and told us that Grandad was dead. Just like she had told us it was okay when he died – leaving out every single detail of how his death was anything but okay. How could have she left it out? How could she have lied about something like that? How could she have made me be the only one to *have* to know?

There was this movie playing out in front of me. I could see Mom and Dad were going to move in to hug Emma, to say it was okay. That it was over.

But in my head there was a different movie. It made everything that was happening in front of me wrong. It was severely fucked up in fact.

Still, all I had to do was let the scene finish. Let the curtain fall. It wouldn't change anything. Emma tried to take her hand away, but I couldn't open mine to let it go.

'Ouch, you're hurting me!' she exclaimed.

'I am not letting you go, Emma.' I tried to stop what I was going to do, to breathe, to just shut up, to stop the pictures starting to flash through my head again. 'They are all lying to you. There isn't a fairy tale ending in what they are going to do to you.'

I turned to Mom. Part of me wanted to stop. To not ruin this. But I couldn't.

'Mom, stop pretending that it is all okay. You know it, and I know it. They're still going to keep pumping her full of poison – what's left of her. One more drug, one more toxic, cell-destroying drug. Look how much good it did Grandad! Look at the bloody mess he ended up to be! You want her to end up like that!'

Looking from face to face, shocked and hurt, I wanted to take back every word. I wanted to cry. I wanted it to be over. I wanted that scene just before the curtain fell.

I couldn't have it. I got pictures of severed limbs and blood splattered rooms instead. I dropped Emma's hand and walked out.

There was one more thing I had to do before I left the hospital. I went into Emma's room, found the DVD of Grandad and snapped it in half.

The problem with leaving like I did, well besides EVERYTHING that was wrong with it, was that now I was stuck. If you've never lived in a village of 423 people, in an area where the trees outnumber the people by, say, billions then you might not know that it's not exactly easy to get from where you are to where you want to go. This is especially true on the weekends, when bus service is almost non-existent. Unless you like taking two days to get there.

I didn't even know where I wanted to go.

At first, all I wanted to do was get as far away from the hospital as possible. I'd needed to calm down, and try to slow the pictures. It was getting harder to make them go away completely, but walking helped. So that's what I did.

My phone rang twice, but I ignored it. I couldn't talk to Mom or Dad, or especially Emma.

I had my mittens, and a jacket. I could just keep walking.

238

I lost time somehow. I'd just kept walking in one direction. I didn't really know my way around Red River, so I just picked a road and started walking. I couldn't remember how long I'd been walking for. The road had kept going, first leaving the businesses behind, then the houses, and now there were mostly trees, and a few houses set way off the road, down long drives. I might have stayed in that comfortable fog, just walking, but the park stopped me. It was empty of people, and there were swings in the corner, behind the baseball diamond. It was starting to get dark and in another few minutes I wouldn't even have seen them. It was a good place to stop and make some sort of plan.

Guilt was setting in now. My hospital stunt had been bad enough, without subjecting Mom and Dad to a day of worrying. What time was it anyway?

When I checked my phone, it was nearly four. Sure enough, there were three missed calls from Mom's phone. No messages from Dell. It really was over. One message from Farley. I opened it. JUST CHECKING TO SEE IF YOU MADE IT TO OKAY.

I rang him back. He answered on the first ring.

'I'm not sure I am totally okay.'

'It's a relative term when dealing with these sorts of subjects.'

'Any tips?'

'I've Kaitlin's car. It's been known to induce laughter. Seems to help.'

'Okay.'

'Where do I find you?' I had no idea where I was. I looked around, for some sort of clue, finally spotting a park sign in the corner.

'Do you have a sat-nav?'

I'd like to say that Farley was there in the next few minutes, but that would have been sort of impossible, since he was in the middle of nowhere and I was in another middle of nowhere. I tried not to think about how cold I was getting. The swings helped. Plus, now that I'd had a few hours to get over the fact that Emma seemed to be fine with letting the doctors cut off her leg, I could get back to thinking about how I was going to make sure that didn't happen.

I tried to recall everything that Dr Jonathan had said this morning. The names of places that treated cancer naturally, the treatments, the statistics of how many got better. I'd taken notes. Or had I shown Dr Jonathan my own notes? It was all a little jumbled to be honest. I'd read so much, written so much down. It was hard to separate what I'd found out on my own from what Dr Jonathan had said.

I tried to put it all on a timeline in my mind, like writing out a history assignment. It wasn't working though. Time was all jumbled up, and I couldn't keep straight what I'd thought and what we'd talked about. It had been today that we'd talked, hadn't it? I could see him, in that halo of light. Only – that couldn't be right. There weren't windows in the basement.

It didn't help that there were so many other thoughts that kept jumping in the way, making it too hard to keep it all straight. The slide show was worse though. Thinking that made me start to feel scared that it was going to start again. *What is wrong with you, Jane?*

I concentrated on pumping my legs, swinging as high as I possibly could. I just needed to wait for Farley. Everything was better when I was with him.

It was properly dark before I saw headlights slowly approaching. I jumped off the swing and ran to the road so that Farley would see me. It was him alright. I could hear the rattling exhaust pipe of Kaitlin's car.

'You were *not* kidding when you said that I wouldn't find the place easily,' Farley said when I got in.

Even with the hole in the floor, the car was heavenly warm. For a moment, just feeling the blast of hot air pouring out of the vent, I felt like I was okay again. You know that feeling, the relief of knowing you are going to be warm again, when you have been colder than you ever have been before?

'So, according to my map of the area, we are nowhere near this village of ill-repute that you live in.'

'No, you're right. I suppose if we were, then I'd be at home by now, huddled under ten blankets to get warm.' Even with the heat blasting on me, there wasn't any feeling in my fingers yet.

'I can get you there if you'd like? Maybe go for a coffee or something, if there's a place for that in Verwood.' He was tentative in asking, like he wasn't sure what I would say. Most of the time Farley seemed so sure that I would succumb to his charm, but then I'd catch this little bit of vulnerability. He was trying to sound casual, like he'd just thought of this, but even in the dark, I could feel the shift.

Could he really like me? I'd thought it was part of the banter between us. But then, I hadn't looked for the signs either. I had been with Dell.

I tried to see his face in the dark, but couldn't. His hands gave him away though. They were always so still, and here he was drumming away on the steering wheel. Waiting for my answer. He was putting himself out there. I could crush his soul with a single word.

'Yes.' I didn't trust myself to say more. All of the fighting thoughts in my head, all of the horrific pictures, were gone, replaced by this overwhelming desire to kiss him. Pure and simple lust. I closed my eyes, savouring the feeling. I wanted to just stay in this moment forever.

We stayed in that quiet as we drove back into Red River. I didn't know I had walked so far. It seemed to take ages to drive, but I wanted it to take even longer. It felt okay to not talk, like Farley knew that was what I needed most right now. Everything was still. Even in my head. Just this feeling of wanting to be here, with Farley, in this moment, with no thoughts at all. Properly feeling for the first time in days. Safe.

I had to talk when we got to Red River though. Farley didn't have a clue how to get to Verwood, and he didn't have a sat-nav.

'But how did you find me?'

He waved an envelope at me, with a mess of lines drawn on the back of it.

'That's your map?'

We'd pulled into a service station so I could have a pee, and now that the spell was broken, I knew that I was going to have to deal with Mom and Dad. I couldn't leave it forever.

'Just let me ring my mom, and then I'll be the navigator,' I said. I rang her before I could think of a good reason to put it off.

'I'm really sorry, Mom,' I said as quickly as I could when she answered, though I knew it wasn't going to erase what I had done.

'Jane, where are you? We'll come and get you.' She didn't even sound angry.

'I'm okay. I'm with a friend.'

'We rang everyone. Tracey hadn't heard from you. Dell wasn't answering. Are you with him?'

'No. Dell and I broke up.' That was for Farley's benefit.

'Where are you? Are you okay? Can we come get you?' I hated how she sounded. I hated that I was doing this to her.

'Farley is giving me a lift home. In a bit.'

'Farley? Who is he?' I could feel that the conversation might descend rapidly into a bad place if I didn't give her what she needed to stop worrying.

'Here, I'll give you his number.' I searched in my backpack for a pen to hand Farley, and mimicked writing as I handed it to him. 'He's nice. He plays the violin.'

When I got off the phone, Farley was grinning at me.

'He plays the violin?' he said, voice full of mockery.

'Well, you do, don't you?'

'And that is the most essential piece of information to relay?'

'Axe murderers don't play the violin, Farley. Every mother wants her daughter to have a boyfriend that plays the violin.'

I noticed that Farley kept grinning as he pulled out and drove toward Verwood.

If we would have just stayed in the car, everything would have been perfect. I might have kissed him. He might have kissed me back. Maybe.

We didn't stay in the car though.

I don't know what I was thinking when I agreed to go into Shirley's for the coffee Farley had promised. I forgot that I live in a village of 423 people. I forgot that it was early December, when nothing is happening and where does anyone go, but Shirley's?

While I'd been trying to keep it together, to think straight, to just get through each hour, each minute, each second, real life was happening for everyone else. Farley was the one real thing for me and I was bringing him to a place where nothing was real for me anymore. A place where everyone thought they knew me, but nobody really did. Do you know what I mean? You see them every week, but they don't really see you?

As soon as we walked in the door all of the thoughts that had stayed away the whole way from Red River came rushing back in. The place was packed with people. A dozen conversations happening all at once. It felt like we were walking into a wall of noise and my mind was racing. I couldn't keep up. And then every face turned our way, and now they really had something to talk about.

I sat down and tried to breathe. It was too hot in here. All of the windows were locked shut and I could feel the hot air pouring out of the vents from the central heating. Half an hour ago I had been a block of ice, and now I was melting. It was difficult to focus with the heat.

I hadn't thought about how Farley would fit into my world here. Hell, I didn't have a world here anymore. Emma's cancer had turned our family into 'a topic'. People thought they were being kind, that they cared. They didn't. They just wanted something to gossip about.

And here I was feeding them some more gossip.

Every head turned in our direction. Every eyebrow rose. Everyone frowned.

Farley was oblivious to all of this of course. Well, maybe not oblivious, but it wasn't his village, wasn't his concern.

Not that I think he would care that everyone was wondering who the hell he was, where Dell was, and what he was doing here with me instead. And it's not like Farley was exactly someone who could blend in. Birkenstock sandals in the winter, hippie jumper — never mind that half the people in the place had only seen skin his colour on television.

I'm not sure how it happened, but our valley seemed to be divided into very distinct regions, keeping the red necks and the hippies as far apart as possible. Verwood was mining and logging territory. It wasn't Kendal. We should have gone to Kendal.

Every word I thought seemed to lead on to a different thought, and I couldn't seem to stop it, to get back to the thought that lead to it.

'Jane, what would you like?' Farley was asking me a question.

'What?' He was across from me, asking me a question and I couldn't comprehend what he was asking me. Sally, who was Dell's cousin, was standing beside me, waiting for me to answer. Why was she there? Was she here to report back to him?

'Do you want to hear the specials again?' She was talking to me. I hadn't seen her come up to us. I hadn't heard her tell us about the specials in the first place. Emma, Emma was special. Why was I here, on some sort of a date, when she was about to lose everything? I'd gotten lost in just being with Farley and forgotten that I was supposed to be making a plan for her.

'A coffee.' I could hear Farley talking, but he seemed far away. I couldn't hear him over the sound system. It was turned up too loudly.

I was so tired. I must have dozed off. I needed the coffee.

'Farley, where's my backpack?' Adrenaline started flooding through my veins with that thought. I looked under the table. It wasn't there. Oh god, I'd lost it and there wasn't time to do all of that research again, to find the answers again.

'It's okay, Jane. I'm buying.'

'No, I need it. I can't lose it. It has everything, all of my research.'

'It's in the car,' Farley said. 'What research? Have you decided to give into doing actual assignments?' I tried to hold his face in focus, but looking at him scared me. His expression was all wrong for the teasing tone he was trying for. Too many furrowed lines, his eyes too wide open with fear.

I really couldn't breathe now. There was this picture of a burning car in front of me. Kaitlin's car was on fire. They were trying to get rid of everything I knew. Burn all of the evidence, keep it hidden. I couldn't lose it. I stood up, heart racing.

'I have to get it. I can't leave it there.' But even as I said the words, I knew that the picture wasn't real. The car wasn't burning. There was no fire. Nobody was going to burn the car.

'Are you okay, Jane?' I wasn't okay, but I sat down, trying to stop this new picture. I just needed to breathe. It would stop if I could just get enough air to breathe.

'I just need to keep her breathing. I forgot. They're all going to stop me. I need to keep them away from her.' In my head, the words all made sense. But they weren't coming out of my mouth right. The thoughts were too fast, half of them getting lost between the words I spoke.

'What are you talking about, Jane? You aren't making sense.' Oh god, I couldn't do this with Farley. Everything was crashing back, and I couldn't stop it. I shouldn't have brought him in here. I was going to lose him.

I put my head on the table, closing my eyes to just stop all of the pictures that were coming back. They wouldn't stop. I put my arms over my head to try to block them.

Inhale, exhale. I concentrated on breathing, just breathing. When the pictures started to slow I concentrated on Farley. He was here, he was real. The only thing I could count on to be real. And when I trusted myself to speak again I told him that we had to go.

We were nearly at the door when they came in it. Tracey, with Dell beside her, and when I looked down, her hand in his. Both of them stopped dead.

'Jane!' Tracey seemed as surprised to see me. I saw Dell looking past me, seeing Farley. I could see what he was thinking.

'I can't do this right now. I really can't do this.' I needed to get out. Now. But Tracey and Dell were still in the doorway and the only way out was between them. Tracey and Dell. They were in the doorway, too close together, and Farley was too far behind me.

'Jane—' Tracey tried to stop me, but I couldn't stop. I was suffocating and I couldn't stop to deal with Farley colliding with my world.

I pushed my way through, separating Tracey and Dell, and leaving Farley trapped. The door shut behind me and Farley was on the other side of it.

The cold air hit me and suddenly I could breathe again. Kaitlin's car was just where we had left it, and it was perfectly intact. Well, at least in the same shape we had left it in anyway. I tried the door. Farley hadn't locked it, and it was still warm when I got in. My backpack was there, covering the hole in the floor. I wound the window down to let the cold air in. I couldn't risk suffocating, while I waited for Farley to get out.

It was taking him so long. I wanted to go and save him, but I just couldn't. What could I do? Every time I opened my mouth terrible things happened. If we had just stayed in the car, kept driving, it would have been okay. I would have stayed okay.

I closed my eyes again, and tried to get back to that blissful feeling of just loving Farley with every thought, every image, every cell. It wouldn't come back. All I could see was Dell, looking past me, and I couldn't see Farley at all.

Finally, after what seemed like ages, the driver's door opened and Farley got in.

'I'm sorry, Farley.' My life was one long list of apologies; none of them any good. I couldn't fix all of the damage I was inflicting. He sat there a moment, just looking ahead, even though you couldn't see a thing out of the front window.

'Jane, tell me what is going on. For you. What's happening?' He turned and took my hand, linking his fingers through mine. I wanted to just think of that, our hands together. Linked. If I opened my mouth, I would break the link.

'Please,' he tried again. 'What's wrong?'

What's wrong with you, Jane? I couldn't think about that question. He was ruining everything. I needed him to stop talking. I wanted so badly to just to be here with him, not talking, not thinking.

There was only one way to make that happen.

He was so beautiful. I leaned over and put my lips on his. Wanting to lose myself in him. Disappear.

The hand that was woven through mine let go, and then both his hands were on my shoulders, pushing me back. Not pulling me in, pushing me away.

'No, Jane.' He didn't even say *Not here, not now.*

And I knew with crystal, clear absoluteness that *this* was real. How could I have possibly imagined that he would want me?

I opened the door to leave. He tried to hold my arm to stop me, but I yanked it free.

'Please don't go.' There was one more thing to say. The last thing.

'Go back to your alternate universe. I don't exist in it.'

I slammed the door as I got out, because that is what you are supposed to do when things are completely over.

Somehow I got home. Somehow I had a conversation with Dad. Thank god it was Dad, Mom having stayed with Emma. I couldn't have withstood Mom grilling me. Not that I didn't deserve it. I couldn't seem to turn around with upsetting someone.

But Dad had been too tired to be upset by me anymore. I

don't even know what we talked about. Nothing I suppose, because even if I hadn't have lost the plot earlier, neither one of us would have wanted to talk about what we both couldn't stop thinking about, what was planned for tomorrow.

I didn't want to think about it. But it was the only thing left for me to think about.

I tried to just sleep. I knew that, logically, that is what I needed to do. And I desperately wanted to sink into nothingness, to sink into a dark pit where I didn't have to think.

When I tried though, it was like dimming the lights in the theatre; all it did was illuminate the pictures that wouldn't stop flashing through my head. They wouldn't stop no matter how tightly I closed my eyes. And now there was nobody I could hope to save me from seeing them, to make me forget them.

I turned on the light and tried to draw, to find the excitement that had been there every time I picked up a pencil in the last two weeks. It was gone. I couldn't make any image stay still enough in my mind to draw anyway.

The research that had kept me focused through the last two nights was finished. There was no point in looking up any more information. Dr Jonathan had already confirmed what I knew, that I just had to stop them from taking Emma's leg. Only, now, in the dark, on my own, I couldn't seem to care anymore. What good was it to have answers, when nobody would hear them? Even Emma was being brain-washed into thinking there was no choice. And when I tried to think about it, I couldn't remember even Dr Jonathan offering to help me do anything different.

Of course he hadn't. He was all conspiracy and secrecy, and no action. There wasn't anyone who was going to do a thing. Not one thing. I was the only one. If I didn't do something, make someone listen, then Emma was going to lose her leg tomorrow.

'Are you sure you don't want to come with me?' Dad was asking me for the third time, as I was nearly out the door to catch the school bus. He was going to the hospital, to be with Emma while she waited for the butchers to take her into surgery. 'The forecast isn't good. There's a storm system moving in.'

I was absolutely sure. I had just finished my third cup of coffee, trying to jolt my mind into some sort of coherent thought, and it wasn't working. I hadn't been able to sleep at all. Even laying still had been nearly impossible and I'd spent most of the night walking back and forth in my room, fighting the urge to go outside. I felt like crying I was so exhausted and fidgety at the same time.

'Dad, seriously, you don't want me there hours before. I'll do your head in,' I assured him. More to the point, it would do my head in. 'Just tell Emma I'll be there. Tell her I've turned the page around.'

I was lying. There wasn't even a page in that stupid book Mom used to read to us for what I was feeling.

I don't know how I thought getting on the school bus would be better. As soon as I reached the top step I knew I was in trouble. The evening before, running into Tracey and Dell in Shirley's, came crashing back into my head. I'd kept the whole mess out of my mind when I'd slammed the car door on Farley. There was too much going on in my head without thinking about Tracey, about Dell, about Farley.

How on earth was I going to keep it out of my head when Tracey was sitting in the same familiar seat? When her posse were sitting right behind her, looking at me like I was about to make their week with whatever came out of my mouth? It was fairly obvious that news had travelled far too fast.

Not as fast as my brain was working though. Not as fast as the words threatening to explode out of my mouth. There was no way I could risk saying a word. As muddled as everything felt, I still knew that I had to keep my mouth firmly shut.

I did pretty well at first, mainly because Tracey didn't want to speak any more than I did. We passed the first half hour with both of us pretending to sleep.

I wished that I could *actually* sleep. I tried to not think, to just see black, to relax even if I couldn't sleep. Tracey's attempt at pretending to sleep, with all of the shifting and sighing she was doing, wasn't helping though. Finally, I couldn't do it anymore and when I opened my eyes to sneak a peek her way, it was exactly the time she was looking at me too, and then we couldn't avoid each other anymore.

'How is Emma?' Tracey was so nervous the sentence came out almost as one word.

'Fine. Well as least five-sixths of her is fine and the remaining sixth won't be relevant after today apparently.'

Well that certainly kept anyone from talking any further. Not even the tag team listening behind us had anything to add, though Tracey looked like I had just slapped her in the face. I didn't want to think about how she felt. I couldn't. I needed to just concentrate on keeping my mouth shut.

But, you've guessed already that I didn't do that. Of course I didn't.

'And how is Dell?' I asked brightly. What the hell was I playing at? I had no idea. The words just spilled out. Four small words that were going to lead to torture for everyone.

Tracey could have spun me all kinds of stories. I could think of several without even trying, all of them perfectly plausible and reasonable. It isn't like I caught them making out or anything. Tracey can't lie though. Not one bit. It's just one of her debilitating, and endearing, features.

'He rang you and rang you, Jane,' she defended. 'I was just trying to help him understand. That's all I meant to do. Honest.'

'So, what did you do instead?' I had no right to do this to her. I knew I had no right. And to be honest, I didn't really care what she had done. It was just ... everything was spinning so fast, and this, this meaningless *thing* was something I could be upset about, could focus on. Or try to anyway.

'You selfish cow!' Brenda exploded, standing up to hoover over me. I swear she had spent the whole bus ride just waiting for her opportunity to say that. 'You were the one who was so horrible to Dell. You were the one who got together with some bohemian weirdo, without even saying one word to your best friend about it.'

It was all so irrelevant to anything that mattered, and Brenda was still standing up, looking almost demented with anger – that I couldn't help it. I started to laugh. Not just chuckle, but laugh, like you do when you *know* you shouldn't, but can't stop. I was laughing so hard that tears were rolling down my cheeks and my sides started to hurt. But it wasn't like laughing when something is that funny. My emotions were upside down, because I swear I would have cried if I could have. If I could have just slowed things down to be able to know how I felt.

She was right. Every word true. And it didn't matter. None of it mattered.

'What is wrong with you?' Brenda said in exasperation. Even though Brenda asked it in the snide, insulting way, I still didn't want to hear it one more time.

'Do you really want me to start, Brenda?' She looked back at me defiantly, and when I glanced at Aishling, her expression was as steely. Even Tracey had her arms crossed, though she looked more uncomfortable than angry. They *wanted* me to start talking.

And that is when I could feel. Anger so sharp that you could cut someone in two with it, which is what I was going to do. 'I can't stand any of this anymore. I can't stand any of *you* anymore. You all sit there looking at me like I am the devil and do you know why? It's because you don't know the devil. You haven't met him. Dances, la de da. New shoes, ooooh nice. Let's all marry our boyfriends and live out nice little lives in our nice little houses. Try looking at half a head lying on the floor. Try fighting the whole pharmaceutical industry that is stealing your sister. I'm not the devil. I'm the archangel and you don't even know it.'

The words exploded around my head. I was glad I had said them. They needed to be said. These girls thought that everything that was going on in their world was so absolutely right when it was actually one big lie.

Wasn't it? It didn't matter because there wasn't any way that I could get myself back to that world even if I wanted to. I didn't know where I was, but I was certainly miles down the rabbit hole from there.

The bus had just made the turn into town and instead of carrying on down the main street, it pulled over and stopped. I realised that I was standing in the middle of the aisle and it wasn't just the three girls who had been listening to me. The whole bus was quiet and all eyes were turned my way. Everyone was against me, trying to stop me. Stop me from what?

'You four girls get off,' the driver bellowed back at us. 'This is your stop today, and if I hear that sort of carry on again, you'll be walking from Verwood.'

I knew then that I had really stepped over the line. We'd had the same driver since starting secondary school, and this was the first time he had ever kicked anyone off.

'You're kidding! I wasn't even saying anything,' Aishling complained. All of us stood up to get off though. I got to the front first.

'Let them stay. It's my fault,' I said. I could see him hesitating. It was starting to snow properly, obliterating the view out the windshield.

'One more chance,' he grumbled. 'Go on. Back to your seat.'

'I'll get off,' I insisted. There was no way I could go to school anyway. I wasn't sure there was anywhere I could go to be okay, but school was definitely not on the list.

I stepped into the swirling snow. Big, wet snowflakes were already sticking to me. Dad had been right; it didn't look like the snow was going to let up for a while. I tried to think of what I should do, where I should go. There wasn't anywhere safe anymore.

Thinking wasn't going to help me. I couldn't even try to keep anything straight in my head. It hurt too much. I couldn't fight whatever was happening any more. I had to give in to where the universe was throwing me and trust that it would work out.

To be honest, I don't remember how I made my way from there to Red River. It was like time started to speed up so much that even though the thoughts and pictures in my head were going faster than I thought possible, I still couldn't keep pace. I know I didn't take the bus, because the CCTV footage showed me walking in the front door of the hospital at 10am, and there wasn't a bus that would have gotten me there by that time. I've kept that fact to myself though; Mom worries enough about axe murderers without telling her I probably hitched a ride, but I can't remember it.

I do remember waiting for Dr Jonathan. Well, I wasn't waiting for *the actual* Dr Jonathan. I was waiting for his signal, to tell me what the plan was going to be. Somehow by that time I knew that he had a plan to take Emma out of the operating room, while she was sedated, and before they cut off her leg. All I had to do was to wait for some sign of where to go to meet him.

And the signal did come. Suddenly, the thoughts just came into my head of where to go.

I know it sounds crazy, and this is really as much as I can relay in a way that even remotely makes sense. You know when you have a dream that completely makes sense when you are dreaming it, and you can still remember it when you wake up, but when you try to tell someone about it, you can't really put it into words? All of a sudden it doesn't make sense anymore? That time was just like that.

I'm told that I paced around the lobby for about half an hour before I went back out the front door, into a raging snow storm.

That is pretty much the last thoughts I remembered before everything turned white.

PRESTISSIMO SALTANDO A TEMPO

'AS FAST AS POSSIBLE; TO JUMP, TO DANCE –
AND RETURN TO ORIGINAL TEMPO'

I am dancing. I can't even tell you what the music is that I am dancing to. Something fast, with a strong beat. And then it changes to some floaty, ethereal sort of thing.

I have never felt as entirely right as I do right now. I could dance forever under this curtain. Just me in the music, in the cotton surrounding me, so that even if I fell, it wouldn't hurt. Not that I am going to fall. I am floating. Gravity means nothing to me. I am pure, perfect movement.

God, this must be what it must be like to dance like Emma. I could dance like this forever.

The light is so beautiful.

I've been letting the softness surround me, and it's so thick that it has blinded me without me noticing. This softness is the warmest blanket I have ever felt. But now, there's this light piercing the dark and the curtain is falling through it, dancing a dance I have never seen before. I need to get closer. I need to see that.

I can see a million universes when I look up. Falling, falling. A million different possibilities landing on me. I had no idea. It is more fantastic than I ever thought possible.

'Jane. Jane. Jane.'

Someone is calling my name. Is that my name though?

'Come on. Get up, Jane.' I want the words to stop. They're making it so difficult to drift. 'Oh, fuck. Fuck.'

I didn't know Farley could swear.

And then I am being lifted up, but I don't want to go. I am screaming and kicking the hands that are taking me out of this perfect universe. I know I will never find it again. *'Please, please don't make me go.'* That is all I am thinking, but I hear my voice saying more. I can't even understand the words coming out of my mouth anymore.

'Drug use?'

'I don't know.' Mom's voice is shrill with panic.

'No, I don't think so,' Farley is saying.

'History of mental illness in the family?'

'Yes. My father had manic depression all of his life.' That is Mom.

And then there is nothing.

I wake up crying. I think I cry for days. It seems like it. Sometimes Mom is there. Sometimes Dad. All I want to do is cry and sleep.

There are doctors and pills. Every time I wake up, there are more pills to take. I don't want them. They're trying to poison me like they poisoned Emma. Thinking of Emma makes me cry again. Have they killed her?

I think I throw the medicine at them. So they give me injections instead. Everything blurs and fades.

I start to take the medicine they hand me. I still don't like it but maybe it isn't so bad because the terrible thoughts and pictures are gone and I know I will sleep again. I want to sleep forever because now that the pictures are gone there is nothing but sadness stretching out in front of me like an ocean.

I can't exactly say when it was that I started to be me again. It wasn't like waking up from surgery or anything. I remember being nine, when I had my tonsils out, waking up, that feeling that I had been dead for days, not just asleep.

This wasn't like that at all. It was more like slowing down a clock, over days. Slowly I started to be able to think at the same pace as the world. Much more slowly, I began to feel 'normal'. I can't say that I started to feel good – because I didn't. I felt more horrible than ever. But apparently this was 'normal'. They kept the world blurred and on mute while that was happening.

They. The doctors. The ones that came to see me. Me. Not Emma.

It took me awhile to understand that *I* was the patient. That it was me that was being treated and not Emma. Well, she was being treated too, but in the *actual* normal part of the hospital — the part where you didn't have to be signed in to visit. We were in different worlds.

They explained to me over and over what the drugs were that I had to swallow. Lithium. Risperidone. The drugs that would slow the thoughts. Things were not right in my brain. I needed to rest; to give the drugs a chance to work.

I wish I could say that I was fixed up in a jiffy, that I was delighted to be getting treatment, that I took it on the chin and got on with getting better. That would be a massive lie. I can't even joke about that time yet. It was the most horrible six weeks of my life.

Think about someone telling you that everything you'd felt, and even thought some of the time, might not be real. Think about someone telling you that your brain needs a complete tune-up, and might need medication forever. As much as I *knew* my head was completely messed up, it was still *my* messed up head. I didn't want it to be changed. Not even when it was torturing me.

And even when I gave in, and the drugs started to work, it was still awful. Worse actually, because then I could fully appreciate how off the wall and how horrible I had been. There had been some fuzzy gaps, but it wasn't like I didn't remember what I had done over the weeks before Farley handed me over. Unfortunately the drugs they were giving me couldn't erase any of it.

The memories of that hospital stay are not ones I want to revisit. I definitely don't feel the need to share them with anyone.

But I can't get away with just moving on either. When you land yourself in the psychiatric ward it isn't like having a broken leg. Stuff happening in your head seems to require talking about it – not necessarily to get better, because, let's face it, talking about being crazy isn't going to fix it. That's what the drugs are for.

It does require coming to terms with how your brain works though – in my case, how it may always work. After a few times of talking to the therapist, I started to see that it might be useful, that I might not be able to get through this without help. I mean, who in their right mind (ha! A little joke) convinces herself to stop remembering that she found her grandfather with half his head missing? I might need help to stop myself from hiding those sorts of facts from myself, so that they don't explode into nasty pictures in my head.

Not that I wouldn't have had other, imaginary images explode in my head apparently. It would have been conveni- ent to blame it all on Grandad, but the only thing I could really blame on him was the bad genes.

More about that later, but I suppose what I want to say is

that when I started telling you my story, I didn't want it to be about Emma's cancer. It wasn't a look-at-the-sick-kid kind of story. And it still isn't, even if the sick kid is me and not Emma. Though, to be honest, it was going to take me a little more time to realise that.

MODERATO TRANQUILLA MENTE

'MODERATELY, CALMLY'

It felt weird that it was me that Dad was driving home from the hospital and not Emma. I almost had a little laugh about it actually, but I stopped myself because my family was still a little sensitive about 'inappropriate emotions'. How many times though, had I had the self-indulgent, dramatic thought of *It should be me in that bed!* I had kind of fulfilled that.

I wished I could share that irony with Farley. I hadn't heard one word from him since I'd slammed the door in his face more than six weeks ago. Well, technically I had heard him when he came and found me in the park, but that didn't really count.

'You and Mom probably deserve a medal or something, Dad,' I said when we were half-way home. I think the guilt was the worst thing about everything. I knew that there was no way I could take away the hurt I had inflicted on everyone, but I had this almost compulsive need to try.

'Yep. You are probably right,' Dad said, but he was smiling, had been smiling since we had got in the car. 'Do you want to nominate us?'

'Well, there is the slight problem of Bipolar Disorder not being great material for gaining public support. Not like cancer does. So, you know, I don't really add to the family adversity in a public way. You probably want to keep the whole mental illness thing under wraps.'

'Jane,' he said, taking his eyes off the road a moment to look me squarely in the eyes, 'I don't care what the public view is. And I don't need anything more than to have two healthy, happy daughters.'

'I can't wait to see Emma,' I said, and god I meant it.

She met me at the car. Emma came out, without Mom, using her crutches like a pro. Seeing her negotiate her way down the icy walkway, still nearly obstructed with last year's untrimmed hedge, made me so proud.

Proud. That is a weird feeling. It really is like your heart is swelling when you feel it. I had been paying attention to feelings lately. This was a new one.

'Ems!' I jumped out and pulled her into a hug, her crutches falling off her wrists and clattering to the ground. 'Oh, I missed you so much.'

We were both crying. I know that sounds completely clichéd, but we were. They don't put these sorts of scenes in movies for nothing. I hadn't seen her for more than six weeks and that had never happened before. I guess it's easy to have the luxury of hating your sister when you can see her every day. Try not seeing your sister for a few weeks; see if you can keep being a cynic.

Dad had to pick up the crutches and reattach them to Emma before I could let her down. This isn't any fairy tale ending; she only had one leg. She would have fallen over if I had released her from our hug without the crutches in place.

Mom was in the kitchen making dinner when we all went in. For a moment, hearing the classical music station she always listened to when she cooked, it felt like the last years had been a dream, like I could blink and forget that anything bad had ever happened in our family. When I walked into the kitchen and took in her whole profile, carrot peeler in hand, hair greyer at the temples than even the last time I had seen her, a mask of fatigue hiding how pretty she was, I knew that it was all real though. The drugs couldn't stop me from seeing every new line on her face.

She smiled when she saw me, but it wasn't like Dad's wide-open grin. She couldn't look at me like nothing had happened. I understood.

I'd known that Mom and I would take the longest to reconnect. That would have been the case if I had never gotten ill, and there had just been The Thing with Grandad, as I had taken to calling it, between us. Loads of time sitting around the psychiatric ward, with nothing more to do other than think, had made me come to that conclusion. Maybe we were too similar, both kind of too intense.

The guilt was the worst with her too. I mean, here she was stuck between generations of craziness. *You are not crazy*, the psychiatrist had said. Even Dr Jonathan had stopped in to try to tell me that.

'Hey there, Hamilton Sister Number One,' he had said, coming into my room sometime after when I was too doped to string a sentence together and before I was certain enough that I could say more than a few words without sounding crazy.

'So, you are real,' I had said. The weird thing was, even though I pretty much knew what was real and what was not by then, I still had clear memories of all the bits that I had been told were not real. It wasn't that I had been completely delusional, but my mind had kind of skewed things to suit where it wanted to go. I think that might be worse than being completely out there, because it makes it a whole lot harder to trust your judgement.

'As far as I know, I'm real,' he had said, pinching his arm as though that would prove it to me.

'But you never made plans with me to take Emma off to some miracle-cure place.' I had pretty much had that confirmed by the psychiatrist, but I'd still kind of hoped that he was wrong.

'I wish I knew of a sure-fire miracle place, Jane.'

'So all of my research was just a bunch of crackpot conspiracy theory.' That had been the biggest let down, that I hadn't been able to save Emma's leg. Nobody had directly told me that surgery had gone ahead at that point, but they hadn't told me it hadn't either.

'I've thought about this a lot.' He had looked kind of sad when he said this, and it had made me feel bad, like I had caused that sadness. As I said, there were acres of guilt to wade through once my mind had slowed down enough to process things. 'Maybe I shouldn't say it, because it might be more confusing, but I'd feel wrong not saying it.'

Then he stopped, and didn't say anything at all.

'What? Say what?'

'The truth is, I am a little sceptical of the way we are treating cancer. I'm afraid you may have been sensitive to my own unease. That wasn't fair.'

'But I *was* out of my mind for a while there.'

'Maybe, but I don't think you were totally wrong. Ok, the internet may not be the most reliable source of information, but it's not unreasonable to question things in life, Jane. Even when you are mood stable.'

'Thanks for that, but I don't think anyone wants to hear opinions from the crazy contingent, Dr Jonathan.'

'Hey, just because your neurons happen to need a little help to regulate, doesn't mean you are crazy.'

Yah, right. I have a feeling Bipolar Disorder is on the list of Crazy Diseases.

I thought it was definitely the reason that Mom hadn't wanted to talk about The Thing with Grandad while I was in the hospital. I get it. Who wants to bring up something horrible, with someone you are afraid might flip out? I suppose it seems safer to talk about fluffy, happy things.

Only thing is, even though I was still getting used to being crazy, I was pretty sure that talking about happy, fluffy things wouldn't keep me from getting depressed or manic again. And likewise, talking about horrible, horrendous things — like The Thing with Grandad — wasn't going to make me crazier. Talking about it *was* the only thing that was going to bridge the gap between me and Mom though.

It was Tracey who came over to see me, not Dell. I didn't expect him to. Even when we were together he had never come over to my house. Also, like I said at the beginning, he had never been someone to face anything difficult head on. I'd liked that when I had difficult things that I wanted to avoid right alongside him. That hadn't worked for me in the long run though. It probably wasn't going to work for Dell either.

At some point he was going to have to stand up to his father, and at some point he was going to have to process the fact that his mom had left him to do that on his own. Maybe that was just the therapy talking though. When most of your human interaction for weeks is with a shrink, you start to psychoanalyse everyone else too. Maybe lots of people go through life not ever facing the bits in their life that haunt them. I suppose if the bad things don't make you crazy, that's fine.

Whatever Dell did or didn't face wasn't going to be my concern though. At least he would have Tracey to help him through, if avoiding stuff got too hard to do. She was a rock. I swear she would have been in to see me in the hospital every day if she had been allowed. She hadn't been though.

Instead, she had messaged me every single day. Mostly she had sent funny pictures and video links, because how many times can you ask someone how they are doing? At first, I hadn't even replied to her most of the time. It had been too hard, and there wasn't anything that I could say. It didn't stop her though; she just carried on contacting me, not asking for one thing from me.

We went to my room now, even though my room is pretty much the size of a closet. There wasn't anywhere else. The house seemed so full with all of us home. It felt like ten of us were living in it instead of just us four.

'Wow, what happened to your room?' Tracey asked. It

hadn't gotten any bigger, but Mom had done an amazing job of redecorating it for me. As far as I can recall, she must have found it literally covered in notes and photos and drawings. Not in a good way either. None of the photos and drawings were gone, but she had organised them for me in a real portfolio, and she had framed some of the best. They were hanging on my newly painted lime-green walls.

'Mom did it. I kind of like it.' I actually loved it. I especially loved the high stool and architect desk she had squeezed into the corner. She had done it as a surprise, but when she had shown it to me, she hadn't mentioned my drawings or photos at all. That had been the best gift. Maybe she had learned from Emma. Sometimes encouragement feels far more like pressure.

Tracey sat down on the bed carefully, like she was afraid she might mess it up. When had we become so formal? We had spent hundreds of afternoons here just hanging out, doing not much at all, stretched out on the bed, eating sweets and throwing the wrappers on the ground. That was before Emma got sick though. Correction – that was before *I* got sick though, because I knew now that it hadn't been normal to stop wanting to be with your best friend, while you waited for the world to just end, almost hoping it would just end. Not at that intensity. Not for that long.

'I have to say this, Tracey.' I wanted to say it right away, because there was no point in her feeling all awkward for ages if she didn't have to. 'You have no idea how much you sticking by me helped. Really helped. But you don't have to. I understand if you want to just spend time with other people instead.'

Saying that made my heart hurt a little. It was the right thing to do though. Farley had never contacted me again. If he couldn't handle me, I could hardly ask sensitive Tracey to stay friends with me.

'Are you mad at me? Because I'm with Dell?' She looked like she was going to cry.

'What?' I hadn't expected that; I was so far beyond it that I had forgotten that Tracey might not be. I'd meant *any* people but me, but she'd heard 'Dell'. 'No, not at all! Honestly, I am so happy for you two, Tracey. It's a two-for-one-deal. My best friend gets the nicest boyfriend, and my favourite ex – well only ex – gets the girlfriend he deserves.'

'Really? You aren't just saying that, and secretly mad?' Knowing Tracey, she had been torturing herself with worry for weeks.

'Come on now, when did you know me to keep any thoughts to myself?'

She laughed, kicking her shoes off so she could sit cross-legged on the bed. Seeing her make herself comfortable in my room, comfortable with me really, made my eyes tear up with gratitude. Gratitude. There was another subtle emotion to think about. I'd kind of resigned myself to the likelihood that nobody outside of my family was ever going to want to be near me again.

'So, tell me about Farley,' Tracey said. 'I hope I get to meet him soon, under ... less awkward circumstances.'

I shook my head. I thought of making light of it, but it didn't feel light at all, and I didn't want to be alone with that heaviness. 'He's over. I haven't heard from him at all.'

'Oh, Jane. I know I only met him for a couple of minutes, but he was so worried. It seemed like he really cared about you.' She got it. I suppose that's what best friends do — they get you.

Tracey and I were going to be okay.

I don't know if Mom would have ever brought it up. Probably she would have had to talk about it in the family therapy sessions that were going to start when my doctor deemed me officially stable enough to work on 'maintenance' as she called it. That sounded ominously like I was never going to be free of Bipolar Disorder. I still didn't like the idea of having this crazy label hanging over me forever.

I didn't want to talk about The Thing with anyone else there though. It was between Mom and me — period. It was our burden and no one else's. Nobody else had to live with

what we had seen. But until now we had both been living
with it alone.

It took me another week to find a time when Mom and
I were alone. Emma had insisted on meeting the principal at
the Secondary School for her tour of the school on her own,
without Mom. She wasn't even close to finishing treatment,
but she was determined that she was going to be there the
first day of spring term. So much for my excuse for skipping
classes. It would be kind of difficult to claim I was visiting
my sick sister if she was in attendance at my school. Not that
I was likely to get away with that anymore anyway. Routine
seemed to be something that everyone was insisting on.

'And don't forget to ask about where you could lay down
for a rest if you needed it?' We were in the school parking
lot, and Mom was going to make Emma late while she tried
to think of every last thing she should ask.

'Mom! It isn't kindergarten. I will be fine.' It looked like
she would be. I didn't know where she had found this determination – maybe now that she wasn't going to dance again,
she had just transferred it to other matters. It suited her
though.

'Don't forget. She'll have me, if she needs it,' I said. Though
to be honest, I felt like I might need her. Only, I'd be back in
school the next week and Emma wouldn't start for another
two months if all went well.

'Okay,' Mom conceded, though she still got out of the car

to help with the crutches and she stood outside the car until Emma had made it up the walkway and had disappeared through the front door. I knew it wasn't easy for her to let her baby go.

We were out of Kendal and on the way to my appointment in Red River before I got up the nerve to talk about The Thing. There was no point in approaching it softly.

'Mom, you know that I saw Grandad first, don't you?'

She turned so pale that I was a little worried I shouldn't have said it while she was driving. I didn't want to do this to her at all, but ignoring it wasn't going to make it go away. I'd tried that.

'Oh, Jane.'

She just drove for a few more minutes, not saying anything more. Her knuckles started to look like wax she was holding the steering wheel so tightly.

'I remember that afternoon every day,' she finally said. 'I was terrified for you. I rang and rang and you didn't answer. I didn't want you girls to have to know.'

'I'm sorry, Mom. I thought the home care lady would find him.' I was crying now. 'I didn't want to be the one to tell you. I couldn't talk to you until I was sure it was done.'

'When you didn't say anything, I wanted to just believe you when you said you didn't go that day. I couldn't, still can't, face that you did.' Her words were stilted by her effort to not cry.

'It's okay, Mom,' I said. 'Well, it isn't okay, but it's better with you.' And it was. Even if she hadn't have been driving I'm not sure if we would have collapsed in a crying heap or anything as cathartic as that, but the curtain of deceit that had separated us was gone for good.

'I should have known. I should have been there for you, Jane.'

'We should have been there for each other.'

She nodded, still holding back the tears. Like I said, it was going to take some time for Mom and me to really be okay, but we made a start that day.

'Jane, there's someone here to see you,' Dad called. I didn't think too much about who that could possibly be, which is probably a good thing or I might never have gone to the door. It was Sunday, and I was fully in dreading-school mode by then, almost counting the hours I had left before I had to face going back to 'normal' life. How was it ever going to be normal again, when I wasn't ever going to be normal? I hadn't factored mental illness into the list of possibilities for escaping the norm around here. It wasn't what I had in mind in any case.

So I guess I was kind of in that self-absorbed feeling-sorry-for-myself mode instead of anticipating who was there to see me. The meds had put an end to my ability to think of more than one thing at a time unfortunately.

There he was, looking pretty much as I had imagined him for the past two months. He had put on some less in-your-face hippie clothes, but there wasn't much he could do about that hair. He looked so perfect and I just wanted to keep this image of Farley at my door framed in my head forever. I'd tried so hard to put him out of my mind because it made me so sad I could hardly stand it, and yet now, even if it was the last time I ever saw him, I didn't want the moment to end.

'You're here.' I stated the obvious. I hadn't thought I would see him again. I knew he had been the one to find me in the park outside of Red River, but who wouldn't have stepped up to help find someone missing in a snow storm? It had been something he would have done for anyone. It didn't change things. If anything, it made them worse. There was no way he was ever going to forget how crazy I could be. He'd seen the worst.

'I'm here.'

I just waited, because this wasn't my visit, it was his, and I didn't know what he wanted from it.

'Do you think I could come in, or even better, do you think you could come out?' He had that vulnerable look, but I didn't know what that meant anymore. I'd certainly read it wrong in the past.

'I don't know,' I said. The half-smile he had given me dropped. 'I mean, I have to ask.' The days of doing what I wanted, without parental pre-approval were over – at least for now.

'Two hours maximum,' Dad called out from the living room, having obviously been eavesdropping. 'School tomorrow.' As if I wasn't acutely aware of the fact.

I was surprised to find a sporty little red car parked outside when I grabbed my jacket and followed Farley out.

'What, did Kaitlin decide to buy a car that is actually road worthy?'

'Nope, but I thought if I was going to take the plunge and stick around here, I had to stop borrowing hers.'

My heart jumped just a little, but I silently told it to calm down.

Farley seemed to know where he was going, as he drove through the village to the main road and then turned in the opposite direction from Kendal.

'You know there's nothing in this direction, don't you?' I said.

'Perspective, Jane. It depends on what you are looking for.'

'I don't know what I am looking for.' I wanted to add *I am crazy, remember?*

'Sometimes it isn't what you are looking for, it is what you find when you are not looking for it.'

'You seem to have all of the answers, but you and I are

living in different universes.' I wasn't angry about it. I was just kind of sad. 'I wasn't what you were looking for, and I wasn't what you found, was I?'

'Is that what you think?'

'It's the only thing I know, Farley.' I'd spent a lot of time thinking about it. 'I may have seemed interesting, but that was only Crazy Me.'

I was remembering the perfect afternoon we had spent together, when I had felt so wonderful, when everything had seemed possible. I knew now that it had just been the beginning of mania. My brain had tricked me into thinking Farley and I had some kind of special connection.

'You were exactly what I needed to find – but I feel so bad that it was at your expense.'

'What do you mean?'

'I was so interested in you, that I forgot that I was kind of messed up myself. I thought if I just lost myself in you I wouldn't need to do my grieving after all. I was wrong.'

'Your mom.' I had kind of forgotten about that.

'My mom, my grandparents, my lost connection with half of me. I wasn't as together as I might have seemed most of the time.'

'I saw the cracks,' I said. 'There are worse ones to have.'

'You have no idea how much that meant to me. I so needed someone who wasn't trying to keep me on some sort of pedestal,' he said.

'Yeah, well, I've had years of practice pulling my sister off hers.'

'The problem was, you were there for me, but I wasn't there for you when you really needed me.'

'There isn't exactly much you could have done.' Which wasn't true. Every bit of it had been better with Farley – for me though, not him. 'But I wasn't real. It was pretty obvious that you figured that out.'

'That's not why I stayed away, Jane!'

'No?' It seemed to me a perfectly logical reason to stay away.

'No. I realised that coming here in the first place wasn't going to make everything better. As nice as Kaitlin is, she isn't my mom. She only really knew my mom for a few years anyway. And my grandparents? Well, you know what a kick in the teeth they were.' I had to smile thinking about Bill and Helen's expressions, standing outside their orderly house, listening to my disorganised spiel.

'And then there was the whole Orchestra thing. I couldn't put off deciding what I was going to do with that too much longer.'

Everything he said was making sense. Still – he'd pushed me away. There was no denying that. I had thought of that kiss, or non-kiss every day, and there was no other interpretation possible.

'When I came here, I expected that something serendipitous was going to happen, that would make everything easy. That didn't happen. I had to go back home for a while, to be honest with my dad, to make the decisions that fate wouldn't make for me,' Farley continued. 'I'm not going to Boston.'

'That must have gone down well with your dad,' I said. As annoyed as I had always felt when Farley started on his 'the stars brought us together' kick, it hurt now to hear how wrong he'd been.

'He'll get over it.'

'But you are here.'

'For awhile anyway. I've got some work lined up on the ski hill. I needed to come back just for me – with no expectations,' Farley continued.

'Well, I'm glad you came back for just you.' I *was* glad for him. It seemed like I was glad for a lot of people who weren't me lately. I understood his wanting to meet me to apologise though. I was doing a lot of that myself.

Farley had turned onto a small road, and after a few metres we came to a little car park, with one of those brown parks' signs saying 'Angel Falls'. We were only a few minutes from Verwood, but I had never been here before.

Farley got out and I followed. I may as well see this through. It seemed pretty apparent that it was going to be a goodbye.

'Come on.' He took my hand and led me up a path. It was covered in snow, but there was an icy trail, where people had obviously been treading. I wished my hand in his didn't feel so right. He did have beautiful hands.

It was only a five minute walk before we came to the waterfall. It wasn't massive or anything, but frozen as it was, it was stunning. A river captured in a moment, rivulets seemingly frozen in mid-drop, revealing exquisite hues of blue and green, stilled so that you could see every detail that would be impossible to see when it was in motion. It was five minutes up the road from where I lived and I had never seen anything like it.

'I take it back,' I said.

'Take what back?'

'Nature and the outdoors not being my thing. I may have been wrong.' I had an itch to take photos. I hadn't picked up my camera since the snowstorm day. Even though I had been home from the hospital for a week now, I had been too afraid to use it, in case it somehow triggered the bad pictures in my head again.

'I knew you would like it.' Farley was grinning again and I wanted to reach up and trace the laugh lines around his eyes with my finger. I wished I could.

'I'm sorry, Farley.' Would I ever run out of people to apologise to? Mostly though, I was feeling sorry for *me*. Being here with Farley was making me remember how happy I had been, even if it had been a little snapshot of happiness, and I wanted that back so badly.

'What are you sorry for?'

'I'm sorry that everything interesting about me wasn't real.'

'All of it was real!'

'No. It's Bipolar Disorder you were hanging out with.'

'Jane. You here today, you in the depths of cynicism, you at the height of happiness – it's all you. You are right, some of it scared me – but that is because I didn't know what was happening, and I wasn't okay enough myself to deal with it.'

'But it can come back. I don't know that it won't happen again – even with medication.'

'Jane, even at the very worst, I could see you. Under all that you were going through, I could see you. You are real.' He had spun me around to make sure I was looking at him when he said it.

'More hippie shit?' I asked.

Farley just kept looking at me, like he had that day on the bus, when I had started to simply let myself be, to stop censoring myself. Now I couldn't seem to find any words at all, and yet, I got that same feeling, like he was seeing the core of who I was.

'This is going to take a while isn't it?'

I couldn't help grinning, just a little, because I was pretty sure this wasn't a good-bye after all.

'What is?' I asked.

'Waiting for you to put some of that ice around you again, you know, so you can put me in my place when I start spouting too much hippie shit.'

'Maybe.'

'When you do manage it though, can you leave a few chinks, so I can get in?'

'Maybe.'

Now, just in case public displays of affection are not your thing, I'm warning you to stop reading here.

'I wanted to kiss you back that day, you know,' he said. 'I just knew that you were too sick. And I wanted to kiss you somewhere magical, like here.'

All of the possible responses to that disappeared before they made it anywhere close to my lips. There were no right words.

'Come here,' he said. 'I mean, if you would like to.'

I did. I knew what was coming, and even though I didn't have one bit of protective ice around me, I did want to. I wasn't sure I wouldn't get hurt. I wasn't sure that I knew what I wanted or needed. I wasn't sure that Farley would stick around if I got sick again.

Everything was one big possibility, maybe good, maybe bad. But sometimes, either way, you just have to take a chance and trust that it might lead to something interesting.

THE STORY BEHIND PLAIN JANE

I've always written as a way to understand the world – and my part in it. It isn't that I find the answers through writing, but when I put words down on a page, my questions about life become clearer; the angst that comes with being a human being abates. I'd like to think that everyone has something similar to make their path through life less cluttered.

And so, when I begin to write a new story, a new novel, it starts with a question or two. Sometimes these are questions I have carried with me for some time. *Plain Jane* started with two questions.

The first question was one I had run away from. Years ago, while attending university, I volunteered on the children's ward of a hospital that specialised in oncology. Twice a week I went in to do arts and crafts with the kids, and quite a few of them would be there for weeks or months at a time. Many were from towns and villages hours away.

I loved getting to know these kids, most of whom took their illness in their stride, dragging their IV poles behind them. Some of them were pretty sick though, and soon, twice in one month – children I had gotten to know died.

That I could handle, though it was sad. The part I found too difficult at the time was seeing the families of these children in the weeks before their dying. Parents were exhausted, many travelling huge distances and juggling the needs of their sick child with those of their other children. And those other siblings – when they were present – were often almost 'ghosts'. The focus wasn't on them – they were going to live after all.

I didn't stick with that volunteer position for very long. I wasn't ready to face such harsh realities on a regular basis. But the possible stories of those siblings never did leave me. How do you cope if you are the 'well' sister? At a time when you are maybe sorting out who you are, where you fit, how does an experience like this impact you? It was something I wanted to explore.

The second question had to do with an illness with a much different public face – mental illness. Cancer has a 'brave' face; it's something you can fight against. Mental illness – when it has a public face at all – is still too often seen as dark or pitiable. I wanted to explore how it might *really* feel to be developing a mental illness. As a writer, I am most interested in understanding life from others' perspectives and experiences, and though in my professional life I have had quite a bit to do with mental illness – that is not the same as getting into someone's head and seeing what the world looks like from there.

I honestly don't know if I captured that experience. Only those of you with bipolar will be able to tell me how close I have come to that goal.

It turns out this book isn't really about what I thought it was about though. I thought I was writing about a girl with undiagnosed bipolar disorder, who has a sister struggling to overcome cancer. It seems that I don't know what my books are about until they are written.

Though I've been fortunate enough to enjoy good mental health so far and was also spared any close encounters with childhood or teen cancer – when I reached the end of writing this story, I was surprised to find my own experiences and struggles strongly reflected in it. I am from a town much larger than Jane's village of 423 people, but growing up I felt the same disconnect between what my peers seemed to aspire to and what I felt – at a gut level – was possible. Like Jane, I didn't know what the alternatives were; I didn't have anyone to give me any hints. It wasn't until I moved from my home town that my gut feeling for wanting something 'more, different' began to take a tangible shape. I wasn't lucky enough to meet a 'Farley' before then.

It took me a while, but I've been fortunate to meet a handful of 'soulmates' in my life, who have been a mirror for who I am. They have illuminated parts of me that I somehow knew were there, but couldn't articulate. My one piece of advice to you would be to keep open to meeting these rare souls. You'll know them when you see them; they will be the people who make you think, 'Yes! You really do see me. That's the person I am!'

At its heart, this book is about the bond between two sisters. I really didn't think it was. It is only in the final stages of editing that I see how central the relationship between Jane and her sister Emma is to the book. I have two sisters myself, and like Jane and Emma, my sisters and I are all very different from each other. We have grown up to live busy lives in three very separate places – and though I think of them daily, I don't tell them enough how much they mean to me. That can be the way, can't it? There is this dichotomy between the people who mean the most to us, also being the ones we take most for granted. Maybe, just maybe, this book is a reminder from my subconscious of what really matters – family, in all its imperfect and complicated guises.

FINDING A VOICE

KIM HOOD FRIENDSHIP IS A TWO-WAY STREET ...

Shortlisted for the YA Book Prize

Jo's got used to keeping her head down and getting on with things.
Between looking after her mother and avoiding the mean kids at school,
she's never had much time to think about what *she* wants – and it
wouldn't occur to her to ask for help.
She has to be the strong one, always.

When she meets Christopher she wants to help make his life better and
will go to dramatic lengths to do so.
But she finds out that friendship is a two-way street ...

A moving and compelling story of friendship against the odds.